"Hutchison takes readers on a stunning, emotional journey with a character you will remember long after you accompany him on his quest for justice. "

~ Carol Costa, Author of
The Secret of Eastman Springs and
When Nothing Else Was Right- Open Books Press

"From the tense, thrilling introduction of the eponymous main character, through a tender love story, and to the heartbreaking revelations of motive and consequence, El Cascabel is a riveting read. Sharing the harsh but soothing beauty of the Southwest, this well-researched novella will have you looking for more of Mary Ann Hutchison's books.

~ Ashleen O'Gaea, Author of the *Coyote Song Coven* series
Available through Amazon

"M. A. Hutchison crafts a suspenseful tale of a young man's descent into murderous madness in the Old West, weaving a rich tapestry of love, loss, and vengeance amid the desert's stark beauty. This is a twisting ride the reader won't soon forget."

~ Jude Johnson – Author of
Cactus Cymry (nonfiction) Open Books Press and
Dragon & Hawk; (fiction) Champagne Books

For my family and friends, with love.

Cascabel
Treachery's Reward

M. A. Hutchison

Open Books
PRESS

Published by Open Books Press, USA
www.openbookspress.com

An imprint of Pen & Publish, Inc.
Bloomington, Indiana
(812) 837-9226
info@PenandPublish.com

www.PenandPublish.com

ISBN: 978-0-9852737-3-6

This book is printed on acid free paper.

Printed in the USA

TABLE OF CONTENTS

ONE

HANK JOINS HIS BOYS

El Cascabel (Spanish for the rattlesnake) was a part of daily living in the mid-1860s Southwest. Cowboys or settlers, cattle or horses—neither man nor animal was safe. No one suspected murder when death visited, with snakebite as a calling card.

The black mustang snorted fearfully, his body rippling with apprehension at the heart-stopping sounds of warning rattles. His ears swiveled, attempting to locate the snakes' whereabouts. Turning his head toward his left flank, he sought reassurance from his rider.

Buster gave that assurance, "Easy, Amigo. Easy, boy. That last gust of wind set them rattles off. It's okay now. We're almost there. Not much further. One more night ought to do it."

The rider turned in the saddle and looked back at the body lashed to the travois. He righted himself before saying, "Hank's not as heavy as the last one. He's easier on you, old pard."

Pulling the neck of the devil's duster tighter, he hoped to ward off the approaching night's chill. The horse whinnied its anxiety at the dry rustling sound the duster made—a sound not unlike the scurrying of dried leaves scattering in the wind, crackling and hissing at the dusk. It had taken a while to create this long coat, sewn from emotional pain and wrought with evil intention, but it was worth the effort.

As the corpse bumped behind him toward the gullet in the earth where the others waited, Buster Johansson mentally replayed the past five of his twenty-three years. He'd done this a thousand times before. He couldn't escape the images that sickened him, plagued his mind, hardened and twisted his soul. Once, he had been a hardworking young farm boy with a family, now his man's work was killing, and he was good at it. Those memory kaleidoscopes made the time pass quickly. As they glided into his mind, he'd briefly focus on a picture. If it was too painful, he'd skip it and look at the next one.

To escape the torture of his losses, he forced his mind to turn to Lonely Wind, his Apache rescuer and only love. Did he still love her? He wasn't sure if he was still capable. The only survivor of a raiding party, she'd found him half alive near the ashes of his life in northeastern New Mexico Territory, transported him to her home in eastern Arizona Territory, and tended his wounds.

As the months passed, his body healed and his psyche hardened. Parts of their days were spent learning each other's language. Sometimes he wouldn't speak for days, brooding in silence. Eventually, she'd learned why he howled with rage one day, and was consumed with grief the next.

Through his sobs, he'd describe how everyone he loved had been taken from him so brutally. The telling did not ease his pain. Even her body provided only a temporary sanctuary.

When he was physically able, she had shown him the place where he would shelve the bodies of the men who had destroyed his life. It was there that his plan had begun to take shape. He wanted no cross to mark his enemies' graves. Later, that same place would shelter those with whom he had found peace and love.

Chapter One

When a man begins sinking into insanity, his mind can become extremely creative. Obsessed, Buster concentrated on methods of death: he needed to take ungodly pleasure in the sights and sounds of their dying; he wanted the cause of their demise to be unexpected, as unexpected as the deaths they caused; and, their last days to be slow, unbelievably agonizing—beyond allowing them time to regret their actions committed savagely on that day over five years ago.

It wasn't merely tit-for-tat; they had stolen lives, they had taken innocent blood, and they had made a pact to lie with the devil. But before they met that old burning man, they would experience living hell—forged from the tears of a young boy, whose family had been taken from him in a senseless act of violence.

He dismissed using a hanging rope or bullets—death would come too quickly. The mutilation factor of knives was intriguing, but again, death might arrive too rapidly. He didn't know much about bottled poison, or where to get his hands on it for that matter. Then one day, he witnessed the death throes of a rabbit as it lay dying after being bitten by a rattlesnake, and it became clear to him how his enemies must die. Death by serpent was the answer.

The strike of the serpent would send poison flowing in their veins and terror into their hearts. The dying would be slow and agonizing—a perfect way to exact his revenge. *El Cascabel* would do his killing for him.

It took time to find, kill, and fashion the eleven diamondback skins that formed the duster's six-inch by five-foot panels. But time was on his side. He used deer sinew to sew the panels together and attach its fur lining. Using the same ligament, the rattles fashioned an easily removable band for his hat. He became serpent; his spirit became *El Cascabel.*

As he crafted the bizarre garment, one picture was branded in his mind. One picture drove him as he would drive the cattle that would lead him to the men who had made his life hell—the looks on their faces as they lay dying.

TWO

THE LAST VISIT

Hunkered by a small fire, chewing a strip of jerky and slowly sipping a cup of coffee, Buster prepared to bed down for the night. The mustang grazed nearby, nervously avoiding the travois parked downwind.

"We're close, boy, we're close. Good thing, huh?" he cackled. "Hank's gittin' a bit ripe. I took the band off the hat so's the rattles won't make ya nervous no more."

Throwing the coffee's dregs onto the forest floor, he stared into the fire. Rubbing his left shoulder, he tried to knead away the dull ache that was a constant reminder of the bullets that should have killed him. The loss of blood would have, if Lonely Wind had not been curious about the column of smoke she saw rising above the trail ahead of her. Thinking of her caused pangs of loss and longing to stab into his gut; her long black hair framing her olive-skinned oval face, almond shaped dark eyes, high cheekbones and full lips floated in the flames of the fire.

Tonight, he didn't want to feel pain, he wanted to feel the satisfaction of another job well done.

He spun his thoughts to the cattle drives that aided his mission. Except for location, the drives followed pretty much the same pattern. Starting at sunrise, he and the others would ride flank or drag, urging the cattle forward, chasing down strays, hoping to make twenty miles further than the day before. They'd inhale dust, especially when riding drag, and fret about stampedes. After getting to a bedding ground for the night, they'd eat, trade a few stories, and catch a little shuteye before taking their turn at night herding.

Buster liked night herding. He'd sing and hum to keep the cattle soothed, watch for lightning; listen for thunder or the cry of wolves—anything that could spook the herd into a stampede.

While he drovered, he'd search for any of five men: Crazy Bill Slocum, Tom Rafferty, Eli Taylor, Ned Howe, and Hank Jensen. With one exception, he wanted—he needed—Hank the most. When he'd locate one, doing the only thing any of them knew how to do, he'd hire on for the drive and befriend his prey. At the end of the trail they'd collect their pay and celebrate as cowhands do, drinking and raising hell in the saloons and brothels of the cow towns where the drives terminated.

One by one he found them as they moved cattle between Kansas and Texas; one by one he cut them from the human herd. He knew where the sixth man was. He wouldn't have to go looking for him.

Eli Taylor was the first. Buster ran across him in a Texas bar at the end of a drive. Because he was the first, and his predator was still a novice, Eli's end may have been the more brutal. As the method was honed, the others' deaths came easier—not to the dying, only to the perpetrator.

Each death began before the victim awoke. Once conscious, he'd find himself bound from foot to neck in his own bedroll, feeling the effects of the drunken stupor from the night before, mixed with a side order of snake venom. The pitching travois heightened those effects as it rocked over irregular earth.

Chapter Two

The chosen was never alone in his bedroll. Attempting a getaway, an imprisoned and angry rattler would repeatedly strike at the object blocking its exit. Compounding each man's fears were the facts that he couldn't think of a reason for his present situation, nor could he recognize his captor. Later, the glow of a campfire would reveal both.

As the sound from the rattles on Buster's hat came closer, each man would hysterically whip his head from side to side, arching his body backward, trying to see how many snakes were heading his way. Slowly, what appeared to be almost six feet of serpent moved into his blurring vision. But the apparition was not crawling on the ground, it was walking upright, as a man—a man shrouded head to foot in diamondback skin.

In the brief time that followed, as each realized he was near to meeting his Maker, he'd come to know the identity of his captor. He'd beg and plead for Buster to finish him off with a bullet. To a man, every one of them named all involved, telling Buster why Cranston had ordered it done, and confessing it was Hank who'd organized the how and when. Then, Cranston paid them off, warning them never to come back to the New Mexico Territory. After splitting up, they'd find a drive and never see each other again.

Hoping to lessen his guilt, each man foolishly placed part of the blame for this horror on Buster's father, saying that if only his father had sold Jupiter to Cranston in the first place, none of it would have happened.

None of them ever understood what the treasured Jupiter had meant to the family. It wasn't only the Hereford's superior bloodline that the Johansson family prized. He'd symbolized the sacrifice the family had made in order to obtain the red giant whose bloodline ran back to the famed Cotmore, the show bull out of a breeding herd in Albany, New York, who'd weighed in at 3900 pounds. Jupiter easily carried over 4,000 pounds and was the bedrock of their future in the Southwest He was the axis on which everything revolved. Jupiter, plus hard work, plus a little luck, would give them the life they dreamed about. Selling him to Cranston would have been unthinkable.

Just before each one gargled his last breath, in an act of coward's redemption the dying cowboy would give up any knowledge he'd had of the whereabouts of those remaining to be found. Crazy Bill added one piece of information that shortened Buster's task: Ned Howe had drowned in a rain-swollen, fast-moving river while attempting to untangle his horse from submerged tree branches.

When the last exhale indicated that death had come to stay, Buster opened the neck of the deceased's bedroll, allowing the instrument of death to crawl away. The bedroll's top was then slid over the dead man's eyes and tied securely at the top of his head; making a nice, tidy package.

Should the trio run into a stranger on the trail, if asked, Buster had his story ready: his poor brother had suffered an accident and was being returned to the homestead for burial in the family plot.

Although he'd practiced the story many times in an unhappy voice, speaking from a sorrowed face, the fabrication was never used. Buster's route kept possible contact with others to a minimum.

Eventually each body reached its final resting place, where it awaited the arrival of the next member of the murderous crew.

THREE

HEADING FOR CRANSTON

It was there on a late autumn afternoon that Amigo now stood, free of his burden. Hank's body was tied securely to one end of a twenty-foot rope. Buster held the other end, slowly guiding it into the cavity, making sure that the now-swollen package would not catch on the ledges lining the interior.

When the parcel hit bottom, he let loose of the body rope, then followed it into the opening using another rope that was attached to the mustang's saddle horn.

Amigo stood firm and waited patiently as he had three times before, listening for the faint sound of a familiar whistle, and two tugs on the rope. Those were his signals to move backward and haul Buster to the surface.

Fifteen feet below, in the glow of a lantern, Buster placed Hank's body into a recess carved into the back reaches of the catacomb. Created centuries before by an ancient Indian tribe, it was the place that Lonely Wind had shown him, a place where she also waited—a secret place in Arizona Territory. A little over a century would pass before it would be discovered near a small town not too far from the Arizona-New Mexico border.

"Say howdy to the boys, Hank. Crazy Bill's layin' in front of your feet, Eli's layin' behind your head and Tom's just above ya. You could reach out your hand and almost touch him. Oh, but you can't do that, kin ya?

"If ya don't already know, Ned won't be joining' ya. He drowned. I bet ya woulda preferred to go that way, too. There's jus one more comin'. You be patient. He'll be here."

If it weren't for these one-sided conversations, the silence of the tomb would enshroud him, causing him to sweat in the uninterrupted cold of this hidden graveyard.

Walking away from the evil lodged on one side of this hollowed core, Buster snaked his way around and through limestone columns to where Lonely Wind silently waited, wrapped in deer hide and nestled on a bed of soft bearskin, a small bundle cradled next to her. He set the candle lantern alongside the spare that was always stored near her. A bundle of matches wrapped in an oilskin lay close; another dozen were tucked in his vest pockets. He placed twelve more tallow candles next to the thirty-six that were already there. He never wanted to be without plenty of light sources.

Buster sat down on the dank earth. Removing his gloves, he rolled a cigarette against his right knee, scratched a match on his rough trousers, and lit his smoke. It masked the odor and calmed him at the same time. Then, he began telling his love about his latest find:

"Ya shoulda been there, Lonely Wind. Ya woulda . . . no, you prob'ly wouldn't have found it as satisfyin' as I did. He was the one, darlin.' Cranston ordered it, but Hank's the one who did it. He confessed it and he's here now.

"And boy howdy how he begged an' pleaded for me to help him die. He was hurtin' an' he wanted me to shoot him and put him out of his misery! He was hurtin' for sure.

"But then, a strange thing happened, honey. All of a sudden, in the middle of his beggin' for mercy, he got the weirdest look on his face. Just afore he breathed his last, he got this look like he had a secret he wanted to tell, but wouldn't, and he said that I'd find out. I told him there were nuthin' *to* find out. That I knew all I hadda know about what he done. That he needed to shut his bazoo. Then he laughed. Honest to God he laughed. He told me I'd find out. That I didn't know everthin'. That I'd see. It were really odd and strange, Lonely Wind, truly odd and strange. A dyin' man laughin' like he did?"

Buster continued speaking to his beloved, finding the sound of his voice comforting in the eerie quiet of the crypt. He never had become used to the dead silence.

Reminding her that he had only one more round-trip to make before his task was complete, before he'd be able to come home to stay, he rolled another cigarette and sat quietly, immersed in his thoughts.

Whether it was because he wasn't quite ready to leave the last family he would ever have, or whether the telling would strengthen his resolve, he described the horror of that day to her again:

"Ma began beatin' on her big jam-cooking kettle and hollered out, 'C'mon all you lazybones, up you get. Today's a busy day and I don't have time to waste.'

"That pot put out a terrible clang an' there was no sleepin' once Ma started banging' away. I always loved it when Ma started the day that way. She had enough energy for all of us an' she didn't abide laying' about. But she was smiling as she was yellin.'"

He dropped his voice in reverence. "I miss Ma. Bad.

"Ma prepared such a good breakfast that mornin'. She cooked up some pieces of ham from the pig we'd butchered a bit ago, an' there were eggs and biscuits and Ma's brambleberry jam and coffee. The house smelled so good, just like good homes should.

"Pa led us off with the morning prayers and asked God for our good fortune to continue. Yeah. Imagine askin' God for continued good luck and then that happens?"

Buster paused, finished his cigarette, rolled another, lit it, then continued, "There ain't no God, Lonely Wind. How could the God Ma and Pa prayed to all the time allow what happened next to happen? It makes no sense, honey. No sense at all. Your Apache God is different honey. Seems to be anyway.

"But when Pa finished with the prayers he didn't commence to eat right away, he just set quiet for a spell an' looked around' the table at us. He sometimes did that. Most of the time he didn't say anything'. He'd jest sit an' grin at us an' we knew he was happy and proud of his family.

"Ma scolded him, sayin', 'Paul Johansson, quit wasting' time. There's chores to be done. Hank'll be back from town soon with the seed and I want that corn planted an' them rows ready for the vegetables. Today! The plowin' ain't gonna get done by itself, an' there's a coupla heifers to brand, an' it's laundry day and them kettles are heating' up an' the water'll be ready right quick. Time's a'wastin.'

'You all better have your dirty clothes in a pile so that Tillie can start bringing' 'em to me a pile at a time. Hank better have that material I ordered for Tillie's bedroom curtains so I can get those started.'

"But she couldn't help grinning' right along with Pa.

"Pa said, 'Clara, slow down. It's not like this family doesn't know what hard work is. Who brought us out here from

Minnesota, who cleared this land, and who built this log house just to suit you Madam Queen?

"He always called her 'madam queen' or 'my lady' an' she called him her Prince Charmin'. They loved each other, Lonely Wind. Just like you and I do. They went through tough times, too. Just like we did.

"Pa said, 'hush woman,' but he wasn't mad at her. They never did get mad at each other. For long anyhow.

"'I'm feeling' too good this morning' to allow you to nag on me. Soon as I say what I wanna say, Buster an' me'll get on with it.'

'Well then get to goin,' Ma said. 'Meanwhile, you young'ns commence to eatin' so you'll be done when Pa's finished recitin' our accomplishments.'

Ma knew what Pa was going to say. He'd said it often enough. 'We left Minnesota in 1858, when you was jest eight Buster, and headed west in one Conestoga and one covered wagon with no particular destination in mind, other than some place in the west so's we could begin life on the new frontier.

My darlin' sister asked, 'And I was . . . how old was I then, Pa?'

"I teased her, like I always done. I told her she wasn't even a 'was' then. She was still flying with the angels and hadn't gotten down to earth yet. An' she pouted like she always did when I joshed with her if she didn't like what I was sayin.'

"Then Pa said, "Now Princess, you know that your brother's just teasing and if you keep your face that way, it's gonna freeze and you won't be my beautiful little Princess anymore.

"Then I winked at her, and she smiled and winked back and everthing went back to bein' fine again.

"And Pa said, 'Now where was I? Oh yes, I was sayin' the Lord led us through some pretty dangerous territory, then down the Santa Fe Trail, and through His Grace He set us down in this valley.

'He's given us everthing a family needs to build a home, nourish cattle, horses, sheep and chickens to sustain our bodies, and threw in rich soil for planting crops. And He sent us Jupiter, the bull that's going to make us rich. Going to create a breed unlike anything ever seen before.'

"Pa stopped for a minute an' took a long drink from his coffee cup. He looked around the table again and said, 'we're luckier than most and that's why I praise His name everyday.'

Then Tillie interrupted Pa's history lesson and said, 'And He gave you me, didn't He, Pa?'

"Pa told her 'yes, Princess, He did. He gave us you and Buster, the most precious things of all.

"Pa always called Tillie Princess 'cause Ma was his queen. He started to call me his Prince once but I didn't like that much, so he just called me his little Buster.

"Then he looked at each one of us, slow like, as if he was trying to memorize our faces, and he smiled again, sayin' 'My jewels; the Johansson jewels.

'Both of you got your ma's eyes. That blue that's like, like a picture of a jewel I once saw, aquamarine I think it was. Comes from her side of the family. The Nilson side.' I fell in love with her because of those eyes.'

"'Now, Pa,' Ma said, and she blushed in the sayin. 'Not in front of the children.'

"Anyway, Pa got to goin' on and on about how some day New Mexico would be a state instead of a territory an' that's when Ma stopped him.

"Darlin,' I've run Pa's words over and over in my mind. If I'da known they were almost his last words, I woulda paid more attention. But I was just eighteen, justa kid really, an' didn't know no better. An' he'd said all that stuff before so I didn't pay too much attention. Just kind of let him go on and on. Kinda like what I'm doin' now, I guess."

Buster stopped his story and sat silent for a long time, staring at nothing. The candles he'd lit when he first sat next to the woman he'd adored had almost become puddles, so he lit six more. Their light bounced off of fragments of embedded crystal-like material encased in the limestone walls, mirroring the flickering flames and adding unexpected earthly beauty to the horror the walls clutched.

But Buster was unable to appreciate the splendor that the small fires had created. His mind and his sight were buried in the past.

"Where was I? Oh, yeah. Almost to Pa's last words. After Ma scooted us outta the house, Pa began plowin' using those two big oxen we had. He started preparin' the rows for the corn.

"Tillie was sitting near the wash lines, playin' with her calico dolls an' waiting for Ma to tell her what to do next to help with the wash. Ma had braided her pretty, yellow hair into two long braids.

"Oh, Lonely Wind, ya shoulda seen the color of her hair. Like butter it was. Pa said she got that from the Nilson side also. My hair's more like Pa's; kinda brown, kinda blonde. I don't know what color it is really. Johansson hair I guess. And I'm tall, like Pa was. Johansson tall.

"Now why am I talkin' about hair and height? I'm ramblin' on, honey. I just want you to know them. To see them like I do.

"Anyhow, our black and white Border Collie, Duster, who helped herd the sheep an' was always at Tillie's side when he wasn't doin' that, was lyin' right near her, like always. She couldn't go anywhere without his bein' right there to dog her heels an' to protect her.

"I was pokin' the branding iron into the fire, waiting for it to turn to red so's I could put our brand on them two heifers. Pa used a "P" and a "J", back to back, for Paul Johansson. I figured our hand should be back pretty soon. Hank'd been gone longer than usual. He'd always been so, so trustworthy. I couldn't figure out why he hadn't returned

"I watched the road, or what passed for a road, expectin' to see him any minute, drivin' our buckboard loaded with everythin' Ma wanted and everythin' Pa needed.

"But while I stood wipin' the sweat off my face, I looked around at the beauty of the land surrounding us. If I were one of those artist fellers I could maybe have painted what I saw.

"All the colors kinda standing out from each other: the white on the snow-capped mountains, against the blue of the sky, mixed with the green of the grass an' the darker green of the forest full of huge pine and white aspens and pretty yeller wildflowers on the edge of the woods, and the red of them berry bushes Ma used to make jams from. The clear blue-green of the stream where we got our water from and where our herds drank. The colors. Oh, the colors. They were wonderful. I've never forgotten 'em.

"Pa was so right. It was our very own heaven on earth. We had everthing anybody could want or need. We were lucky. I kin still see it. I'll always be able to see it. But then, but then —"

Buster began to cry. He sobbed loudly; his sobs turning to moans that reverberated throughout the tomb.

Then, as suddenly as he'd started, he stopped. Taking deep breaths, he returned to normal.

"I'm sorry for the noise Lonely Wind. But when I remember what came next—those sounds, the voices. I kin still hear the voices. I always hear 'em. You know that. Well, that just got me to bawlin.' I know how you hated it when I cried. But I couldn't help it then an' I can't help it now. My family then. An' now you an' our little guy.

"If I tell you again, maybe it'll stop the voices in my head. An' the sounds. Maybe not. I don't know anymore. I'll try.

"I heard the gunshots first. Then the yellin' and the whistlin' of the raiders as they stampeded the cattle, an' the cattle were bawlin,' 'cause they was scared. An' the wood fences in the corrals was crackin' and splinterin' 'cause 'cause the cows were spooked and pushin' up against 'em. They wanted out.

"The noise. Oh, the noise."

Buster put his hands over his ears, and shook his head from side to side, trying to stop the noise. Then he stopped shaking his head, and took several deep breaths before starting again.

"An' then, then . . . then Pa was callin' 'Buster! Buster, run and git the rifle, boy.'

"An' Ma. . . Ma was screamin' 'Pa! Pa! Buster! Buster where are you? Help us, what's happenin'? Tillie? Tillie! Come here child. Come to your ma.'

"An' Tillie, my sweet Tillie, was cryin' and screamin,' 'Ma. Pa. Buster. I'm scared. Ma!'

"An' Duster was barkin' and growlin' and circlin' 'round Tillie. Not leavin' her side.

"An' there were more shots an' then all of a sudden their voices stopped, an' I heard Duster yelp in pain, an' then there weren't no screamin' anymore. No one was callin' my name.

"An' all the while I was hearin' the noise an' the screams I was runnin', Lonely Wind. I was runnin' as fast as I could towards the house. I wanted to get the double barrel shotgun that was jest on the inside right of the front door, hanging on the longhorns mounted in such a way that all ya had to do was reach in and grab it.

"An' I had jest landed on the porch, an' I'd almost reached the door when the first bullet hit me on my left side, jest above my waist, and the second bullet got me in my left shoulder and I fell and skidded an' almost hit the door.

"An' then that's when I heard him. I heard his voice. That dirty double-crossin' son-of-a-bitch'n bastard. Hank. Oh, he wasn't comin' to our rescue. No sirree. He was leadin' the raiders and yellin' instructions:

'The boss wants that monster bull, Jupiter. Don't harm a hair on his red hide. That's one valuable animal. Round up the cows and them calves. Make sure them Swedes is all dead. I don't want them bein' able to identify anybody. Then let's get the hell outta here.'

"I smelled smoke and heard the cracklin' of flames an' I knew our house was burnin'. They'd set it afire.

"Then I blacked out an' I never saw my family again, except in my head where I keep the pictures."

Buster set his mouth in a grim line, slowly rolled and lit another cigarette, took a deep drag, and expelled it along with his next words.

"Ya know the rest of the story, Lonely Wind. Took me five years but Hank's here now along with the rest of Cranston's men. It's good there's only one more to bring in cuz I'm gittin' tired. I left him for last. I needed to find the others first.

"You should see how raggedy the skin on the coat is gettin'. An' it's startin' to smell something fierce. But it'll do for one last wearin'. Then I'll shed it, just like its first owners woulda done. I think I'll keep the hatband, though."

He rambled on a bit, as he always did before shyly telling her that he missed her, how he wished he could hold her in his arms one more time. How desperately he wanted to feel her lips on his and her body close. He'd always been shy when it came to expressing the love he felt for the woman he cherished.

Finally, he said, "I'm a-gonna go now. Swift Wind is waitin' up yonder. Nowadays I call him Amigo.

"I'm bringin' Jupiter an' some of his line back with me an' I'll set up a homestead near the meadow like I promised. Hell, I'm twenty-five. I'm tired of the trail anyhow. What with the wages I took from 'em, an' what I got for sellin' their horses, I got me a nice nest egg." He paused before saying, "They owed me.

"But I won't be gone as long as afore. I won't have to search for the last of 'em. I know right where he's at.

"An' when I get back, I'll build that cabin that we talked about. Yes, I hear ya. It won't be close to where you, to where you died. I'll honor your people's wishes on that one. It'll be up against the forest, and there's plenty of land for the cattle, and everthin' will be the way it once was. Well, almost."

Buster turned and shouted his other good-bye, "Boys, I'm a-gonna go an' round up yore boss. Meanwhile, y'all have a lot to jaw about." He giggled at the thought.

Walking over to the body rope lying on the ground, he coiled it, then attached it to his belt. Wrapping the dangling rope around his gloved hand, he gave it two swift tugs and let out a loud whistle. Leaning forward, he blew out the candle in the lantern he'd placed on a ledge in front of him and looked up towards the light. Slowly, but steadily, he rose out of the blackness and into faded daylight.

When he got topside he stood and inhaled deep breaths of the piney air to rid his lungs of the smell of decay, and watched while the sun sank and the fingers of the moon's first light touched the mountain's top. It rose quickly, and by its light he unsaddled Amigo, set a campfire, and unwrapped his bedroll, handling the oilskin wrapped duster and hatband that was cocooned inside it with great care.

"Only one more trip, old pard. We'll start early in the mornin'. We won't be gone too long this time. We won't be goin' so far."

As if the horse understood every word that was said to him, he stopped grazing on the sweet grass, walked up to his companion, and nuzzled the right side of his face.

Buster reached up and patted the horse's neck. "Yore welcome, Amigo. It's been a long haul. Cranston's probably settin' on his porch right now, admirin' Jupiter and his offspring. An' if the rumor 'bout his drinkin's true, he'll be needin' one 'bout now. He'd prob'ly enjoy bendin' an elbow with someone who drovered with four of his old hands."

FOUR

MEMORIES OF A RESCUE

The next three weeks went by swiftly as Buster rode back toward northeastern New Mexico. The time he'd just spent near his wife and son affirmed the fact that his love for her had not waned, but was still strong.

He longed to hear her laugh, he longed for her touch, for her smile, for her gentle ways, for her strength, for her teachings of a different way of life. She had understood his need to avenge his family's murders. She'd understood revenge. That's what her life had been about.

The time they spent together had been rich and full and were the happiest times he'd ever known. On the day Baby Paul was born, his joy was so overpowering his body had trembled with the awe of what they'd accomplished. Two people had made a third. It was a miracle. It was extraordinary.

Rather than clouding his memories with cattle drives, and the dragging of bodies, he spent the better part of his days in the saddle concentrating on the only treasure he'd ever possessed. His Lonely Wind:

Out of the darkness he'd slipped into on the porch of his burning home, she'd crept into his consciousness by sight, scent, touch and sound: all at once, not separately. He saw, smelled and felt her, but heard nothing—nothing but the quiet of the forest.

Gone were the repeated roar of gunshots, and the sickening sounds of his family's screams. Gone was the yelling of commands by a betrayer; gone was the lowing of frightened, stampeding cattle, gone was the booming shatter and splinter of wood, and gone was the usually pleasant smell of burning pine. Until the day he died, he would equate that burning odor with the loss of the home he'd helped to build and, if he could help it, he never burnt pine again.

Instead, when he'd opened his eyes, he'd looked up and into dark brown, almond-shaped eyes, surrounded by long black/brown eyelashes. They were perched above an aquiline nose and full lips, in between high cheekbones.

Her long black hair was somewhat restrained by a headband that almost, but not quite, covered her forehead. The light brown buckskin band could not stop some of her hair from tumbling onto his left shoulder.

He was lying on his right side and she was kneeling next to him, applying an herbal mixture to his gunshot wounds and abrasions. The compound cupped in her left hand looked a bit like a glob of cooked spinach, but smelled more like cabbage. Her touch was soft and gentle.

He would learn that the yarrow which gave off the smell, and for which she'd search when they looked for food, was used as a cure for wounds or injuries or warding off a myriad of sicknesses.

For now, she'd made a poultice that would clot the blood caused by the bullet holes. Soon, she would make him drink a tea made from it and other herbs that would relieve his pain and help him to sleep.

Chapter Four

His voice cracked as he tried to speak. "Who are . . . what hap . . . where am I? Ma? Pa? Where's . . ."

She'd put a finger against her lips indicating that he should not speak, then placed her free hand on his shoulder, firmly indicating she wanted him to remain on his right side. He complied without further resistance; the pain was too strong to allow him to do otherwise.

As soon as she'd finished with the application, she put a cup to his lips and he began drinking the potion, which was sweet and only slightly bitter.

She helped him onto his stomach and he was vaguely aware of lying on something soft and furry, and very comfortable. He lifted his head in an attempt to find out where he was. Through a thicket of branches, he first smelled their strong aroma, then saw the pine trees and was instantly consoled by the feeling that he was in the forest near his home, and that his memories of screams and fire and murder were just bad dreams.

In that mistaken belief, he fell into a deep sleep.

FIVE

A NEW HOME

In the days that followed, the regimen was the same: he'd awake to the touch of her tending his wounds, giving him small amounts of food and drink, only allowing him to stand and walk a few feet to places where he could relieve himself (after she discretely left the area), then helping him back onto a travois that was the method of his transportation.

The travois was made of three poles lashed to form an isosceles triangle. The sharp ends of the poles faced forward. A piece of leather had been stretched to make a sort of bed, on which a bearskin had been placed for warmth and a degree comfort.

He was not aware of how much time had passed. It didn't matter to him. He was grateful for the drink that brought sleep, a drugged sleep that made him unable to think straight.

Sometimes he had nightmares that made him scream in anguish, and she'd be there to comfort him. She'd calm him by speaking softly, and administer the drink that led him back to the dark land. He never wanted to leave that land, never wanted to exist again. Existing meant surviving and he didn't want to survive.

Then one morning he opened his eyes to find that he was alone. He looked around expecting to find her near, but there was no sign of her or her horse. There were three other horses grazing in a nearby meadow and he recognized them as being part of his father's herd. He felt a rising panic, but when he tried to get up and off the travois, he was too weak, so he lay down onto his back, not minding the pain that sprang to life from his wound sites. He noticed the pain wasn't as bad as it had been.

Through the branches of the large oak he was lying under he saw dark clouds forming in the sky, heard the rumble of distant thunder, and felt the moisture-saturated air; a storm was building.

A gray squirrel was sitting on a branch right above him gnawing on an acorn, eyeing the man below.

"I'm alone and I have no idea where I am," he said to the little animal. The squirrel continued watching him and to nibble unconcernedly.

The indifference of the squirrel made him angry. Rerunning that day and Hank's betrayal made him seethe with rage; longing and grief for his family made him sick to his stomach. He gagged on the bile that rose and, rolling to the edge of the travois, he vomited.

Struggling to a sitting position, he buried his head into his hands, and gasped for breath. After a few minutes, he threw his head back and opened his mouth, laboring to breathe. The sound that emanated from his opened mouth originated in his gut. The keening turned into a long, high wavering sound, a mixture of a wolf's baying and the roar of a grizzly. It was unlike the cry of any animal the inhabitants of the forest had ever heard before.

Birds flew from the trees, the squirrel ran to the end of the branch and launched itself into the next tree, fleeing from the sound, a deer foraging near him turned and crashed through the brush in order to get away from whatever thing was creating that noise.

The orphaned Buster Johansson, baptized Paul Joseph Johansson Junior, was alone in the White Mountains in northeastern Arizona, and alone in the world, and he'd never felt as sorry for himself as he did now; the tears flowed once more.

The hand on his shoulder startled him. He looked up and saw that beautiful face, the face that he'd come to recognize as comforting and loving.

But there was no comfort in her countenance now; rather, there was a sternness about it. There was no smile. Her hands brushed at her eyes, as if she were wiping them, and she shook her head from side to side.

He cocked his head to one side, put his hands out in supplication, and shrugged his shoulders. He didn't know what she meant.

She put her fingers to her eyes, ran them down her cheeks, and again shook her head from side to side.

He put his fingers to his eyes and ran them down his cheeks, and shook his head from side to side, mimicking her gestures. When he felt the tears dampening his finger tips, he got it. "You want me to stop crying?"

A brief smile crossed her lips and she nodded in the affirmative.

"But, I can't. It's too much for one man to bear." The tears came again.

She clapped her hands and this time her eyes crackled with determination; her mouth was set in a firm line. She shook her head from side to side.

He wanted to see her smile again; he needed to see her smile. He made a tent of his fingers, placed them on the bridge of his nose, thumbs on either side of his jaw, just below his mouth, and pushed hard, taking deep breaths until the desire to cry stopped.

She walked to where she'd left her burden basket, sat down and began to sort the vegetables and herbs heaped in it. The skinned carcasses of two rabbits lay nearby. She didn't look at him.

The wind came up and at first the tops of the trees swayed in rhythm with the swirling air, as if the two were performing a tango. As the storm increased so did the intensity of the dancing; the trees bent from the force of the angry wind, and the rain began to hammer down.

She picked up the basket, and walked to where he sat.

He looked up at her, his brow furrowed in question. She nodded her head toward a wickiup and waited while he stood, and after he walked a few feet without faltering, led him into the shelter.

While the lightening crashed and the thunder roared, they were warm and dry in the dwelling that all Apaches call home. It was constructed of arched wood poles and covered with brush, and was easily large enough for at least four people to live in quite comfortably.

Her burden baskets rested on the floor, along with her saddle. Two rifles rested against a wall—one he recognized as the one he was running for on that day so long ago, Parfleches and drinking gourds hung from another wall near her bow, and arrow-filled quiver. Blankets and cooking pots were arranged against another wall. A smoke hole had been placed directly over the fire pit.

Buster sat on the dirt floor and wrapped himself in the bearskin that had been his bed, which he'd quickly snatched from the travois before entering the hut.

They both watched the small fire she'd started for warmth, ate the wild walnuts she'd gathered, along with handfuls of currents, and listened to the storm howling outside.

The combination of warmth, a full stomach, and the feeling of safety, overtook him. He wrapped the bearskin tighter, clutching it to his chest, lay on his right side and soon fell into a dreamless sleep.

SIX

COMMUNICATION

In the beginning, communication was established through simple hand gestures: a finger over the lips meant "quiet," a hand cupped to the ear meant "listen," pointing to the eyes and then to the object to be viewed meant "look."

Although neither would have passed for a great artist, drawings in the dirt by finger or stick worked a little better and the drawing of a deer was recognizable by both as a deer. Thus was hunting and searching for food accomplished.

Buster missed the sound of words, the talking and sharing of a day's occurrences, and longed to be able to speak to her and have her speak back. He had so many questions for her. He needed to know why she was so different than any woman he'd ever known. Although, in fact, the only women he'd ever been in contact with were those in his home-state of Minnesota, those he'd met on the wagon trains, and his ma and sister.

She rode a horse like a man, she handled the rifle, the bow and the knife with outstanding accuracy, better than any man he'd known, she knew the woods as if it were her home, killed animals, skinned them and made clothes and containers from their skins, she knew how to treat wounds and where to find the plants that aided in their healing.

He figured she knew just about everything there was to know about life and he wanted her to teach him what she knew.

There was nothing left of his old life; nothing but sad memories. He wanted to be a part of her life, at least for awhile.

If he could learn what she knew, he could survive and get the revenge he wanted, the revenge he needed. He vowed that he was going to get it as soon as he was healed and whole again. But whole again meant being unbroken; meant being complete. To the end of his days he would always be broken and never complete.

His first attempt at speaking with her occurred one morning after breakfast. Unless communicating through signs or grunts, the two rarely made eye contact.

Buster cleared his throat, but she didn't look up, just continued working on a quiver. He cleared his throat again, this time drawing it out and this time she looked at him, eyebrows raised in question.

Pointing to himself, he said, "I'm called Buster. What are ya called?"

She stared at him, eyebrows furrowed, not understanding.

He spoke slowly, "My name is Bus-ter. Bus-ter. What's your name?"

She shook her head.

"Okay, let's try this. Me Bus-ter. Me Bus-ter."

He pointed at her, "You?"

She shrugged her shoulders, continuing to punch the awl through the skin she was using to form the quiver. She'd shot the mountain lion sometime ago, had tanned the skin, and formed it into the shape of a quiver that would last for many years. It would remain as strong as the beast from which it was borrowed.

He raised his voice. "Hey."

She looked at him again. Sideways. Her forehead furrowed.

"Me. Bus-ter." He pounded on his chest. "Me. Bus-ter.

She cocked her head and smiled. He noticed how beautiful and shiny her hair was when it fell to the side as it did now. He'd spent time observing the sheen of her hair, the shape of her body, and its strength. He'd noticed that about her. Among other things.

She pointed at him and gave one quick, affirmative nod. Her voice held a note of pride as she repeated, "Me-bus-tah." She pronounced the two words he'd used to indicate his name in clipped syllables, ending it by using a long "a" sound with no "r" sounding.

He threw his head back and laughed for a long time. It felt good to laugh again.

"Yes. Me-bus-tah. Me-bus-tah it is. It'll do. It'll do."

She gave out the little grunt that he'd come to recognize as meaning "good." "Hmm. Me-bus-tah."

He looked at her, pointed and said slowly, "Now, you. What—do—you—call—you?"

She shrugged and shook her head. She didn't understand.

He pointed at her. "You. What's your name?"

She shook her head again, this time with annoyance, and went back to work on the quiver, pushing the deer sinew through the holes made by the awl.

Buster dropped his head. The sound of their voices had cheered him. Other than the cries of the birds and the occasional calls of animals, and the arboreal whispers, grunts and groans given off by the trees and bushes, their world was one of quiet. It'd been months since he'd carried on a conversation with anyone.

The sound of the wind blowing against the side of the little house made him feel lonely again. When there was no further conversation between them, he went back to talking himself, so he wouldn't go crazy from feeling alone.

He spoke aloud, softly, expecting no answer. "That's such a lonely wind."

In their early days together, on those occasions when he'd given quiet voice to his thoughts, mumbling as he followed her on their searches for food, she'd watch him carefully, wondering about his mental state. Her knife was always at the ready, just in case he went crazy. Once she'd decided that he wasn't crazy, she'd ascribed it to his being quirky and as there'd been no attempt at talking between them, she'd paid little attention to his mumblings.

"I've got it!"

She jumped. Startled by the loudness of his voice, she dropped her awl, and reached for her knife.

He pointed at her. "I'm going to call you Lonely Wind. Lone—lee Wind. You. Lone—lee Wind."

She stared at him; expressionless.

"Lone- lee-Wind. You. Say it. Say Lone-lee-Wind."

She nodded, then, "Low-lee-win." Same clipped pronunciation, no "d" sound at the end.

"Yes," he nodded. "Close enough. Low-lee-win."

He pointed at himself, "Me-bus-tah." He pointed at her, "Low-lee-win."

She pointed to herself, "Low-lee-win." Pointing at him, "Me-bus-tah."

They both smiled.

She returned to working on her quiver, he got up, picked up a pitch-covered basketry jar used to store water and said, "I'm going for water."

She didn't understand the words, but understood the pantomime, and nodded. "Hmm."

As he headed for the stream, he said, "Mebbe now we kin learn enough of each others' words so's I kin ask her questions and find out about this strange woman who saved my life."

Buster would find out that there was a lot to learn about this woman, this Apache Woman Warrior.

SEVEN

A NORMAL LIFE

As the weeks went by, they came to know an ease of being together.

She'd never known a white man, and he'd never known an Apache—man nor woman.

Speaking English seemed easier for her than the learning of Apache for him. He'd tried to mimic the lowering or raising of the pitch of his voice when pronouncing vowels, along with the nasal quality and the catches in breath that certain words called for but more often than not, he'd end up saying the wrong word and saying something ridiculous, like calling a piece of wood a hat.

He managed to learn that when she referred to her Apache heritage, she didn't refer to herself as "Apache" but rather the term was 'n'dee,' meaning "people."

Eventually, he learned that her true Apache name was Tos-teh-se, but they both referred to her as Lonely Wind. She knew that n'dee changed their names often after birth so it was of no importance to her that her name had become different.

From dawn to dusk, there was never a time of what Ma referred to as 'lazin' around'. Wood and food was gathered, animals were hunted, skins were tanned and clothes and shoes were made.

About a month after they'd settled in, Buster woke to find that, as usual, she'd gotten up ahead of him.

He sat up, preparing to wrap a blanket around himself—his bloody shirt had been thrown away somewhere on the trail between New Mexico and Arizona, and his denim pants had become tattered and the seams split; he might just as well have been naked. He noticed what he took to be a short skirt lying on the ground next to him. He'd seen pictures in his school books and recognized it as a loin cloth.

He put it on, and walked outside to find her.

The fire had been laid, a deer brain was steaming in a pot of water, and she was removing the pegs from a piece of deer hide that had been lying on a grassy area for the past three days.

Buster watched her for a minute or so, then said, "Thanks," and pointed to his loin cloth.

She looked up, smiled and nodded, and then went back to turning the rawhide to buckskin.

He watched with fascination as she worked the brain into a mush, added deer fat to it, applied the pulpy mass to the skin, put everything into a utility basket and worked the skin until it became soft, adding warm water when it was needed.

When it got as soft as she wanted, she hung the dripping skin from a tree branch to dry a bit before wringing it out.

Buster had wanted to help in some way, but his assistance was brushed aside until it was time to pull and stretch the skin, then they worked together and by noon had a beautiful piece of buckskin finished and ready to become a new pair of pants for him.

He would learn that in the Apache life, tanning hides, making clothes, building shelter, gathering wood, building fire, was considered woman's work. Women also learned which plants were used for medicinal purposes, as well as food.

After a meal of nuts and pemmican, Buster went for water (he'd insisted on doing that so he wouldn't feel so useless) while she finished scraping the flesh off of another deer hide using a sharpened deer bone, then spread the hide on a large patch of grass, with the inner side facing upward, and pegged it down.

Two or three days later, after it was completely dry, she would not go through the tanning process she'd just done, but rather would use the thick hide for moccasin soles or ropes. Buster soon wore a pair of moccasins, followed in a while by a buckskin shirt.

His outfit was almost a match to hers, the shirts were the same, but she wore a knee-length buckskin skirt, and knee-high moccasins.

EIGHT

EL CASCABEL

Their life together soon became one of teacher-pupil. He learned how to use the bow and arrow; death came quickly and silently to those it was used on. He became proficient with a knife. He'd always been a pretty good shot with a pistol, a rifle, and a sling shot, but he could never top her accuracy.

But even as he learned, he still mourned. Many of his nights were filled with anguish.

All food was just sustenance and was vastly different than that on which he'd been raised. It had little taste to him. He missed his mother's cooking: her bread, her pancakes, the cookies and cakes on birthday and holidays, her stews and roasts.

He missed playing with Tillie. Even though there was a twelve year age difference, they were close and he'd been her protector. Well, he and Duster. He'd danced with her and played tag and they'd laughed—a lot.

When he thought of those fun times, and how they'd been snuffed out as quickly as one pinched a flame from a candle wick, the anguish he felt was replaced with a hate so strong that he could almost reach out and touch it.

The life he'd known was no more. His life that had begun in St. Paul, Minnesota in 1850, in a roomy two-story limestone house, and had changed into a large, log cabin in northeastern

New Mexico Territory, was now confined to a wikiup in northeastern Arizona.

Although there had been hardships on the trek to the new frontier, his family had weathered them all: climate change, the loss of some creature comforts (they'd had to leave their large sofas and chairs, bed frames and tables and chairs with neighbors in St. Paul) the reports of dangers from hostile Indians (which they'd never had to contend with), trading the raising of vegetables in their backyard garden for growing almost all of their vegetables, raising and slaughtering cattle, a few sheep and chickens, ducks, and geese for food, and keeping a dairy cow for milk and butter, they'd survived that and more as a family.

Now, except for a woman whose lifestyle may as well have been established on another planet, with whom he was just beginning to have conversations, who was better at everything than he, he was alone.

He'd stopped crying, for he knew that displeased her and he needed and wanted her approval. He liked it when she'd smile at him, so he buried his tears inside, covering them up with dark moods and occasional bouts of anger.

He'd been used to helping Ma with things that needed to be done around the house. But now, every time he wanted to help, she shook her head no. Even the simplest of meals meant hard work had to be done first, but he wasn't expected to do it.

When his grief overwhelmed him, he'd take the bow she'd made for him, pretend that he was going hunting and go into the forest and sit and wallow in self-pity and hate.

One day, as he sat motionless, staring into a small, slow-moving stream and as usual reliving that fateful day, he became aware of another of life's battles going on across the water.

Chapter Eight

A cottontail rabbit had hopped its way into hell and lay jerking in death. The rattlesnake, who'd struck without its usual warning, had recoiled and was waiting patiently while its poison did its work and it could unhinge its jaws and slowly swallow its prey.

Buster watched the little animal's agony and a smile slowly crawled across his mouth, not because he was being insensitive to the mammal's dying but rather, because of the snake's method of killing.

Buster had thought hundreds of times about the method of death he would use on his enemies—a gun, a knife, a rope. None of these seemed to satisfy his thirst for blood. He wanted, he *needed* to see each of them die a horrible death—one that was painful; one that took a long time. And during the time it took them to die, he wanted to be able to tell each of them why they were dying.

He knew the faces and names of all of his enemies:

Hank, their trusted ranch hand, who'd lived and worked with and for them, who was like a member of the family, who was following the orders of their neighbor,

Daniel Cranston, a wealthy cattle rancher, whose offers to buy Jupiter—the Hereford bull whose champion bloodline would eventually make all the hardships the Johansson family bore worth every minute—had been rejected,

And the four of Cranston's ranch hands who'd followed Hank's lead.

Cranston would be the easiest to find and kill. He'd always be in northeastern New Mexico Territory. Finding the others would take some doing.

Buster notched an arrow into the bow string and took aim. The arrow flew straight, and quietly, efficiently entered the snake's body between its head and the bulge in its body that outlined the remains of the rabbit. The snake had struck without warning; the arrow had arrived without warning.

"As ye sow, so shall ye reap," he said, sloshing through the stream. As he skinned the Diamondback, his plan became darker.

NINE

THE COAT

In Buster's mind, the day of his rebirth began the day he'd killed that first rattlesnake. He wasn't swwwure why, but from then on, when he went hunting, whether for small animals or large, he'd make a point of trying to find the largest Diamondback he could, purposely looking in rocky areas where they would most likely be.

After he'd collected four of them, he'd hung the skins side by side, staring for hours at the patterns on their backs, intrigued by nature's designs.

"Well lookee there, Lonely Wind. They look just like pieces of cloth dryin' on Ma's wash line."

He was silent for a bit, then smiled and then became jubilant as the outline of his plan began to define in shape, and become blacker.

"Lonely Wind, I know just what I want to do with 'em. But I'll need ya to help, 'cause I can't sew a lick."

From then on, he'd try to make sure that each skin would come as close to five and a half feet in length as possible, so it would stop six inches from the tops of his boots, but it didn't really matter. When he'd decided what they would be used for, he knew those of shorter lengths could be patched together.

TEN

NO CROSS SHALL
MARK THEIR GRAVES

The last piece of the puzzle fell into place on the day that Lonely Wind showed him the place where earlier ancestors had, thousands of years ago, buried their dead.

Little by little she'd come to understand the words he used, and the reasons for his tears when she'd first found him, the tears that had transformed into instant anger and black moods. She understood revenge. It was as much a part of her life as breathing.

Buster had spent another entire evening reiterating the details of how he would search for, and then destroy his enemies.

"The only thing I can't figure out, Lonely Wind, is where I'm goin' to bury 'em. I want every last trace of 'em wiped out. as if they'd never been here a'tall. I don' want 'em to have crosses on their graves, or their people to know where they are.

"I haven't figured out that part yet. But I will. Yessir. I will."

Lonely Wind said nothing; just listened and watched, still unsure if the man she was now sharing her life with, the man who was now sharing her bed, was crazy. She thought he might be, a little bit, yet she was not afraid of him. She loved him. She also believed that one should never be afraid of someone you love.

The next morning she bridled both their horses, threw two lengths of coiled rope and her fringed saddle bag over the front haunches of her mustang, saying "Come."

"Where? Where are we goin'?"

She put one of her decorated pouches around her neck. "Come. You will see."

They rode through the forest for half of the morning, until she reined in her horse, jumped off and tied it to a low branch of a large Ponderosa pine.

She looked at Buster and nodded, indicating that he should do the same.

He complied without question. He'd learned it was easier that way.

Reaching into her saddle bag, she took out what looked to be candles similar to that his ma had made from lye soap, and put them into a pouch she'd wrapped around her waist.

She tied one of the ropes around the trunk of the pine, made sure the knot was secure, and carried the rest of the length with her to roughly twenty-feet east of the tree to where a large boulder lay.

When Buster joined her near the huge rock, he was a bit puzzled to find that she'd thrown the rest of the rope into a large hole in the ground. The hole was roughly six-feet in diameter.

Lonely Wind nodded toward the hole. "We go down."

"What?"

"We go down." She was insistent.

"What the hell?"

"You want to bury enemies? We go down. Now."

"Now justa minute here. I'm not gonna . . ."

"When you see light, hear me call, you follow."

Not allowing him to say another word, Lonely Wind grabbed the rope and disappeared into the hole, lowering herself slowly into the earth, using her feet as guides against the rough sides of the opening.

Not long afterward, Buster heard her voice, "Me-bus-tah. You come. Now."

He peered over the side and saw a light flickering in the darkness about fifteen feet below.

Folding his arms against his chest, he contemplated this next phase of his education with her. He'd climbed ropes upwards; not downwards.

Her demanding voice seemed very far away, "Me-bus-tah. Now!"

"You're not goin' to get one over on me, girl. I'm comin', "he yelled.

Mumbling, "How hard kin it be?" He began working his way down the rope to where she stood, holding two burning candles.

"What the hell is this place? Or *is* it hell?"

He looked up. Seeing even a bit of the sky made him feel a little better.

The candles only afforded as much light as it took to see her and just a bit beyond. They were standing in a relatively large room.

"Where are we?"

"Ancestors' home. From long ago. Follow."

Buster lowered the candle to see what he was walking on. The earth on which they stood was hard-packed. Bones from animals that had inadvertently fallen through the fissure were scattered about.

Columns of limestone stood like sentinels here and there, remnants of the journey of an underground stream that had dried up long ago.

Outside of the small circle of light, it was blacker than pitch; blacker than anything he'd ever known.

He thought that this must be like the inside of a grave, and shivered with delight at the idea.

After roughly ten minutes of fast-paced walking, he started to say, "How much farth . . .ooph . . ."

He'd tripped on something that rolled away from him. When he looked down to find the object he'd stumbled over, he saw a human skull lying about two feet from the end of his right foot, grinning up at him.

"Lonely Wind? Where are we now?"

"Look. This is where you bury enemies."

Buster raised his arms to allow the candle in each hand to illuminate the area.

On either side of the wide path they'd been following, niches had been carved into the walls. Each was approximately six feet long, by three feet wide, by two and a half feet high and had been carved in such a way that it was compartmentalized into spaces that stored three bodies.

Some of the shelves still neatly held the entire skeletons of the bodies placed on it. Others only held a few of the bones, the remnants having fallen to the ground as the possible result of long ago earthquakes.

No matter what the case, the mouths of all of the skulls gaped open, as if singing in an unearthly choir.

"My God, Lonely Wind, how far does this go?"

"Many miles."

"How long has this been here?"

"More moons than stars in sky."

In the silence of the tomb, he heard the last of the pieces of his plan thump into place.

"Thank you, little darlin'. Thank you so much. I love you."

In the limited light afforded by the candles, she could see his smile.

ELEVEN

LIFE IS GOOD

Summer—she called it the "thick with fruit" time—passed into fall. When the leaves turned color, she said it was the time when the "earth is reddish brown."

They began to harvest berries and vegetables for storage to be used during the time of "ghost face."

Berries were picked and either eaten immediately or dried for use in the winter.

They'd leave home for several days and go to the lowlands to find mesquite beans which would be ground into flour or cooked with meat, and the prickly-pear cactus which would be eaten right away or mashed for its juice or dried.

Nuts were plentiful and burden baskets would be filled with them.

By the time winter arrived, they had gathered what was needed and after the first snow fell, much of their days were spent in the warmth of the wikiup, making or repairing clothes or shoes, fashioning Buster's snakeskin coat (the one he would wear only when death visited), or making love.

Their love grew slowly and in the beginning came about as the result of one of Buster's constant nightmares. His screams brought her to his side one night and, as she lay next to him, holding him to quiet and calm him, his body responded in other ways. It was his first time with a woman, but it was not her first time with a man.

Lonely Wind had been married when she was sixteen, four years before she'd found Buster. Her husband had been killed while seeking revenge on a tribe that had attacked their tribe, killing Lonely Wind's father and brothers.

War and raiding was a way of life for her.

As children, along with the boys, n'dee girls were trained in all things, whether they used the skill or not. Everyone was taught to cook and to sew; there might be a time when that skill was needed, especially by those going on a raid.

All of the children were taught to mount an unsaddled horse and everyone but the lame participated in foot and horse races and played at stalking and hunting.

As a young woman, Lonely Wind had been expected to guard the camp and fend off raiders should the men not be around. She was also expected to hunt small game and had been trained in the use of the rifle, knife and bow and had been taught how to escape in case of capture, how to use camouflage, and handle horse.

But when it came time for her to take part in the more traditional female functions, her prowess in tracking, shooting and running allowed her the opportunity to ride with the warring parties, not to cook, clean or care for the wounded, but to fight in the battles.

She'd been highly regarded as a warrior, and had been part of the raid formed to avenge her family. Although she'd fought bravely side by side with her husband, she'd not been able to save his life, and was next to him when he died.

Chapter Eleven

With a ferocity she'd not felt before, she killed her husband's slayer, and although scalping was not a usual procedure, she took her enemy's scalp and placed it on her husband's body, so that all would know his death had been avenged.

She was the raid's lone survivor and in her anguish vowed never to war again.

Instead, after a dream in which she was told to return to the place of her birth where she would die alone, she'd begun the long trek back to the White Mountains of Arizona.

During her way to her homeland, she'd come across a burning cabin, saw the bodies of an older man and woman and a very young girl, lying bloodied on the ground, and saw a young man crawling off the porch of a cabin and toward the body of the little girl.

She was inexplicably drawn to him, for reasons that would become clearer to her later. Placing him on a travois that she'd quickly assembled, she piled a rifle, some cooking pots, an axe and a few other household objects around him, caught three horses that were wandering near the house, and continued toward her birthplace.

All this and more was told to Buster during the long winter months as their ability to speak and understand one another became easier.

TWELVE

THE SAGA OF LONELY WIND

The raucous cries of a pair of Stellar jays caught Lonely Wind's attention. Until the birds' warning calls, she'd been lulled by the loping gait of the mustang into a daydream state – her mind comparing the noise of the battle she'd fought a few days earlier, to the refuge of the peace she was seeking.

Her body became taut with expectation as she notched an arrow into her wild mulberry bow. The birds' cries could mean a warning to the flock that there were intruders in their area. She was the intruder, but was she the only one? The cries could mean there was danger to the flock itself. She needed to determine what the calls meant.

Reining the horse to a halt, she quickly scanned the tops of the Douglas fir and the aspen that formed a canopy above, and cocked her head toward her right shoulder, attempting to define the noises of the forest. Sight, sound and instinct were her protectors now.

The ears of the horse had perked up at the broadcasting cries. He remained still.

The Apache warrior's eyes dropped from the treetops to the floor of the woods; she briefly examined the small stands of ferns between the tree trunks that lined both sides of the rail she was traveling, examining the chokecherry and snowberry bushes that interrupted the greenery for any signs of feeding animals.

Nothing.

The jays' screaming returned her attention skywards. Her body relaxed as she saw the reason for all the noise. A large red squirrel was trying to make his getaway from the bowl of the birds' nest, a bluish egg clutched firmly in its mouth.

Ah, it is different when you're the one being robbed. She knew that jays were notorious for robbing the eggs of other birds with utter disregard.

The squirrel wasn't having much luck dodging the pecks from the diving birds as it leapt from branch to branch, until a well-planned leap onto a particular branch of a fir tree and a fast dash found the squirrel at the mouth of a hole in the tree's trunk. After scurrying to safety, it popped its head out of his nest, taunting his victims with his scritching cries of triumph.

Lonely Wind tucked the arrow back into its mountain lion-skin quiver, placing her bow on her back, next to the quiver.

The lengthening shadows, along with the late afternoon activity of the squirrel, told the warrior that it would be dark in a couple of hours.

This night she was tired. This night she wanted shelter rather than continuing her trek towards home. She was used to traveling at night as it was safer.

After selecting a number of dried branches, she fashioned her wikiup, tied the mustang to the branch of a nearby tree, said a prayer to Usen for protection, and fell into a deep, dreamless sleep.

THIRTEEN

THEIR FIRST MEETING

Aware that she was not alone in her wikiup, Lonely Wind opened her right eye only wide enough to determine if her roommate was a friend or an enemy. She'd fallen asleep on her stomach, on the left side of her face, her right arm tucked between her breasts. Her right hand ever so slowly crept upwards toward the handle of the knife that lay next to the left side of her head. She was ready to spring and defend herself.

Two small, beady, black eyes stared back at her. The little ground squirrel's nose was twitching furiously as it stored the smell of human into its memory. The woman and the squirrel were almost nose to nose. Neither moved.

Apparently satisfied with what it had learned, the furry critter scampered away, continuing its search for breakfast. Lonely Wind blew out the breath she'd been holding and smiled. She slowly rose into a sitting position, listening to the sounds of the forest awakening. The morning birds were calling their welcome to the new day; the rustle of dried leaves on the ground indicated that small animals were searching under them for hidden treasures of seeds and nuts.

Her stomach rumbled its complaint, and she reached for her parfleche. It held a supply of dried meat, dried fruits and walnuts and she ate some of each, making up for the evening meal she'd missed.

She listened to the forest sounds again. Nothing had changed that would indicate danger, so she crawled out from her shelter, gave Horse a pat as she went by on her way to find a place to relieve herself.

Securing the parfleche to her belt and unfastening the reins from the tree branch, she mounted Horse quickly as she'd done since childhood, in one easy, fluid movement.

She began again her long trek homeward to complete her destiny. Shortly after the raid in which her husband died, she had a dream that told her to return to her birth place where she was to die alone. Dreams were powerful medicine and were not ignored. She did not question the reason for, or the meaning of, the dream. If she was meant to die alone, she would not return to her people but would spend her remaining life away from them.

The smoke from a burning cabin prompted her curiosity. Her bow at the ready, she remained in the shadows of the trees at the edge of a clearing; watching.

The bodies of an older man and woman and a very young girl lay bloodied on the ground. No movement from them caused her to presume they were dead.

Movement from the direction of the cabin caught her eye. A young man crawled slowly off the porch of the cabin towards the body of the little girl. He appeared weak from blood loss. There were no signs of other white men.

She was inexplicably drawn to the crawling man. Searching for branches, she assembled a travois.

Poking through the wreckage of the small area of cabin that had not completely burned , she found a rifle, some cooking pots, an axe and a few household items she thought might be useful. She placed those on the travois next to the man. When she caught three horses that were wandering near a corral, she congratulated herself on her good luck. Horses were valuable and were always sought.

Alone no more, she continued toward her birthplace and her destiny.

FOURTEEN

A SON

He learned more about her ways, than she did about his ways, only because when he tried to speak about his family, he'd become morose and severely depressed, so it was better that he not even try.

He was an enthusiastic pupil and eager to hear about the ways of her people, and because of his youth and inexperience eager to practice the techniques of lovemaking, and before the time of "Little Eagles," as she called it, or early spring, as Buster referred to it, Lonely Wind was pregnant.

Lonely Wind was very chaste, and Buster had never seen her naked, but in the darkness he'd come to know every facet of her body. Even though she'd once been a warrior, and he had no doubt that she could return to those ways instantly if called upon to do so, she was lithe and graceful and he loved to watch her move about their home.

He'd noticed that her breasts were becoming larger, and it looked to him as if she'd put on a few pounds, especially in her abdomen, but not having been around many pregnant women, it had never dawned on him that she was going to have a baby.

"Are you gettin' fat, Lonely Wind?" he'd teased one evening.

She smiled. "Why do you ask?"

"Well, yore um, yore titties are gittin' bigger."

"Yes, they are."

"An' your tummy is poochin' out a bit."

She dropped her head, then looked up at him and smiled.

"Um, I never cared one way or the other about a woman's being fat or not. It really doesn't matter to me. I'd love ya no matter what."

"Me-bus-tah. I am not fat because I eat."

"No, no. Don't get me wrong."

Still smiling, she walked over to him, took his hand and placed it on her stomach.

He frowned in puzzlement.

"Feel that?"

"Feel what, honey?"

"Feel your child."

He was silent for a long while, but he kept his hand on her stomach, afraid to take it off. Then the tears rolled down his face once more.

"Are you not happy again?"

"Oh, Lonely Wind, I've never been happier in all my life. I just wish Ma an' Pa an' Tillie were here. They'd be overjoyed bein's as it's their first grandchild and all."

She nodded. "I wish the same."

"C'mon down here woman, an' let me hold you proper like."

He held her in his arms almost all night, but when he reached for her and wanted to make love, she told him there could be no more lovemaking until after the baby was born.

"Why?"

"It safer for baby not to."

"Oh. Well, I guess I kin understand'. It's all right, then. I want our baby to be safe."

"I need to make belt from skin of white-tailed deer."

"Why?"

"It will make birth easier."

"Okay, then. Is there such a skin in that stock of skins, or should I go and kill one?"

"Such a skin is there. I will wear it the next day."

From then on, the Lonely Wind's safety was of utmost important to Buster.

When she performed the normal duties around the house he worried that she was doing too much.

"No, no. Me-bus-tah, that's good for me."

"But yore doin' too much."

"No. I am fine."

He never tired of holding his hand against her stomach and the first time he felt his child move against the palm of his hand he became so excited he hyperventilated and almost fainted.

Lonely Wind too was experiencing elation. She'd never been pregnant before, but had watched the birthing process many times, so knew what to expect.

She took great care to make sure that the child growing within her would come into the world in good health, and that there would be a safe delivery.

It was only the two of them. There would be no midwife to help, and no shaman to pray or sing or perform the usual ceremonies to insure the good health of the baby, but Lonely Wind was not worried about that. She was confident in her abilities.

During an especially heavy snowfall, Buster asked, "When will the baby get here?"

"When Ghost Face finished and Little Eagles almost over."

"That's not help'n me much, Lonely Wind."

"Four moons. About."

"Wow. That long? I want to hold him now."

She laughed, and kissed him. "You good father."

"I know. I think I'll be a good father. Just like my pa." He hung his head for awhile, memories of his father played in his mind, but no tears followed.

Two moons passed, spring chased the winter away.

Buster and Lonely Wind were enjoying a spring afternoon. He was sitting in the shade, and she was lying next to him on a sheepskin blanket.

She didn't sit up as much as she used to. When Buster expressed his concern, she'd told him that it was perfectly normal.

"If I sit on baby now, that not good. He will not come out easy."

She didn't ride her horse anymore, nor lift anything heavy for the same reason. Buster did all the hunting and gathering, but never went far from home for fear something was going to happen to his little family.

"What are we goin' to name the baby?"

She shrugged. "Not important now. Can wait until several moons have passed. It will tell us when."

"I never heard of such a thing. We always name our babies right when they're born."

She smiled. "Call it baby then. Me-bus-tah's baby."

He grinned at her joke.

"How 'bout we call it by my middle name, Paul. It was my pa's middle name, too."

"Paw?"

"Paw-el. Paul."

"Hmm. Baby Paul?"

"Okay, Baby Paul."

"What if it's girl?"

"Then, we'll call it Paula."

"Hmmm." She nodded in assent.

As the weeks went by, Lonely Wind worked on the baby's cradle board. Using oak and buckskin she formed the back of the cradle, with a piece of ash connecting the frame and the canopy. Wild mustard was gathered for the bedding.

She would not cut symbols into the buckskin covering the top of the canopy until after the baby was born. A girl's cradle would be decorated with a full or half moon, and a boy's with a cross or four parallel slits.

As instructed, Buster placed an oak post in the ground at one end of the wikiup. This would help Lonely Wind during labor.

On the first day of June, 1870, Baby Paul Johansson was born after sixteen hours of hard labor.

As was customary, Buster had been banished from their home during the procedure, but remained outside in case she needed him.

But after six hours of hearing his wife's grunts and moans, he went in to help. He'd seen farm animals born and figured there couldn't be a lot of difference.

Seeing her kneeling before the oak post, knees apart, grabbing it whenever a labor pain hit, caused him a bit of anxiety, but he didn't let it show.

She was grateful for his help and between the two of them they managed a skillful delivery. Lonely Wind used a sharpened black flint to cut the cord and tied the end with a piece of yucca-leaf string.

They had a bit of worry when the baby didn't take a first breath and began to turn blue, but when cold water was dashed on the tiny body, Baby Paul reacted by crying loudly and becoming pink.

Two days later, the cradle hung from an oak tree branch, to the east of the wickiup, signifying that the baby with the sparkling blue eyes, who would have been safe in that cradle, had died.

Baby Paul was buried quickly in a rocky slope and covered by rocks, branches and earth.

Three days after that, Lonely Wind again lay on the sheepskin blanket, being bathed with cool water to try to take the heat from her body.

"Me-bus-tah?"

"Yeah, darlin', I'm here."

"I am dying."

"No! No. You. Are. Not. I won't let you."

She took a deep breath. "When I found you, I coming here to die. To place where I was born. A voice in a dream told me. Told me I die alone.

"When I see you, I feel if I bring you with me, I would not die alone. That's why I stop and help you to live. Now I know that to be true. I not die alone."

"That was just a dream darlin'. Dreams don't mean a thing. They can't tell you when you're goin' to die. That's superstitious nonsense."

"Baby Paul waiting. I go to him so he not alone."

"You can't leave me, Lonely Wind. I don't want to be alone. I love you. Please honey. Don't leave me."

Lonely Wind fell asleep in his arms and never woke again.

On June 6, 1870, two years and five days after she'd rescued Buster, Lonely Wind succumbed to the fever that raged within her body.

Buster didn't cry. He sat and held his wife's body for almost twenty-four hours, staring at the walls, not thinking of anything.

Then he washed her lovingly, and combed her hair and wrapped her body in a piece of buckskin, wrapped his sheepskin blanket around the buckskin, then rewrapped it in a piece of buckskin.

He dug up Baby Paul and using a travois, he and Swift Wind (she'd named his horse that after the horse outran her mustang) transported them to where their ancestors lay waiting. The other horses he left to roam free in the White Mountains.

Buster quickly renamed the horse Amigo; it was now the only friend he had. The horse, who'd been trained as a cutting horse, responded to all of Buster's instructions, and in a while mother and son were lying under the earth, in the catacombs.

"I don' want to leave you, Lonely Wind, but ya know that I have to. We talked 'bout it. Remember? We agreed that I'd have to take my revenge and that you'd wait for me until I did what I have to do.

"Only ya were supposed to be on top of the ground, not under it.

"I haven't cried yet, honey. You'd be so proud of me. I wanna cry. I've tried to, but I can't. Maybe some day.

"Our son's here too, so's you two will always be together."

As if in answer, the candle wick flickered and made a bit of popping sound.

Buster smiled. "Thanks for that darling'. I love you too. Got to go honey. They're waitin' for me to help them meet their end. I'll be back. Soon."

As was the custom of her people, he placed all of Lonely Wind's possessions into the wikiup and set it on fire. Following another of her customs, Buster cut his long, brown hair to shoulder length, signifying he was in mourning.

He cried and sobbed for two days, until his blue eyes became steely, his mouth became set in a straight line, and he never shed tears again.

Now, after finding and bringing all of his enemies to the catacombs, save one, he began the ride back to where Lonely Wind had found him, towards northeastern New Mexico.

FIFTEEN

TREACHERY'S REWARD

During the day, he'd picture his meeting with Cranston over and over, hundreds of times:

He'd ride up to Cranston's big house, pretending to look for work. In his fantasy, Cranston would welcome him and they'd get to talking about how he'd come to know Hank and the men who'd worked for him oh so long ago. It would be an innocent conversation and Cranston would never suspect a thing.

There would be no wife, no one to suspect anything when Cranston disappeared.

And as the man he hated, the man who'd made his life a living hell, drew his last breath, he'd say to him:

"Now it will be as if you never lived. You gave nothing to the world but sorrow. No one will miss ya.

"An animal mourns for the loss of kin. No one will mourn your loss.

"Your body will mix with the dirt and nothing will grow from where you are buried. In death, as in life, ya'll be worthless.

"Even animal dung serves a purpose. You have none. So you're less than that which falls from an animal's arse."

He practiced that eulogy over and over again; and the miles passed and he got closer and closer to his quarry.

Over and over he'd picture Cranston's face contorted with pain and remorse. Oh yes, there'd be remorse. And tears. There'd be tears as he begged Buster to spare his life; pleaded for his life to be spared. But Buster knew that his laughter would drown out the piteous whining of the dying man

And Buster would laugh at that thought, and the miles passed and he got closer and closer to his quarry.

Each night, before falling asleep, he'd picture where his final homestead would be built—after Cranston was safely tucked under ground with the others.

He carefully plotted the cabin's placement. At times he'd place the front porch of the house right over where he figured the bodies of his enemies were stacked. That way he could sit in his rocking chair, smoking and rocking back and forth, holding them down, so they'd never be able to leave.

Still, at other times, he'd place the house right over the tomb's entrance, so he could climb down and visit Lonely Wind and Baby Paul whenever he wanted. He'd build a sturdy ladder, too. Nothing was left to chance. Of course, he'd never be able to speak of his plans to anyone.

Amigo was the only one who knew everything, except for Lonely Wind, of course, who was always with him. Anyone else would think he was crazy.

He'd cackle at the thought that anyone would think he was crazy; the voices that were now his constant companions, assured him that he was not crazy.

SIXTEEN

THE OLD HOMESTEAD

Three weeks and a day after leaving Lonely Wind, Buster was awakened by the sound of her voice calling his name. Keeping his eyes tightly shut, he listened intently, but didn't hear her call him again. "Must've been a dream."

Standing, he stretched his arms out and twisted from side-to-side trying to work out the kinks, his body stiff and aching after lying on the rough hard ground all night.

There was a sick feeling in the pit of his stomach. He shrugged his shoulders several times, hoping to throw off whatever it was that was bothering him. Needing to feel the nearness of something he loved, he whistled softly for Amigo. As his only friend loped towards him, Buster surveyed the clearing in which he'd camped the night before. It had been past dusk when he'd decided to bed down but as he looked around, a nagging feeling of recognition wrapped itself around him, adding to his discomfort.

Knee-high weeds and grass were interrupted by scattered, haphazard rows of dried, bleached-by-the-sun cornstalks, some still upright, some broken off and leaning at crazy angles. Stirred by an early morning breeze, they waved to him in a familiar, friendly manner; the sound of their waving was dead and dry.

It was if someone had once planted the rows neatly, and then not tended them anymore, and they'd reseeded themselves over the years; dying and being reborn wherever they wanted.

At the sight of a stack of rotting fence rails piled neatly off to one side, his stomach began cart wheeling, and he dry-retched. He ran his hands through his hair, again and again, then pressed the palms of his hands into his eyes. He didn't want to look anymore. He didn't want to see what was becoming horribly and painfully obvious.

"I need some breakfast, Amigo. An' I could use a cuppa coffee." The horse had resumed grazing, ignoring his friend's pitiful attempt at conversation. Buster turned and knelt in front of his saddlebags. Throwing one open, he retrieved a bag of coffee grounds tucked inside a gray enamelware coffeepot. He lit a fire, picked up the coffeepot and called out, "Amigo, I'm goin' to the stream to get some water for my coff . . ." He stopped in mid-sentence.

"How the hell did I know there was a stream nearby?" His mind played ping-pong with questions and answers:

Musta crossed it last night.

But we came from the other direction.

Naw, ya jus' got turned 'round. That's all. Don't think about it. Jus' go on 'bout your business. Make the damn coffee!

Buster turned and headed in the direction his gut told him to go. He hadn't gone four steps before the sight of what lay thirty feet ahead made him drop the pot. He swayed unsteadily.

"Snap out of it," he commanded. "Jeezus Chee-rist, what's the matter with ya this mornin'? It's not the first time ya seen graves."

Regaining his composure, he began walking toward the two rectangles of earth, outlined just short of the forest's tree line by whitewashed river rock. Little yellow flowers were planted in front of the crosses that were firmly positioned inside the rocks on one end. Normally, those flowers grew wild in the woods, but they had been dug up from their usual home and replanted here.

With calm certainty, he knew where he was. He knew whose names he would see carved into the whitewashed wooden crosses. He stopped within three feet of the final resting places and read the words drawn in black paint, in a child's uneven scrawl:

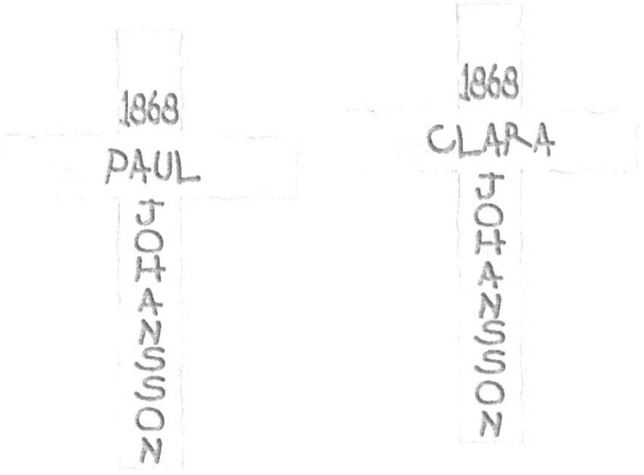

A cattle brand burned into the wood below each name erased all doubt as to who was buried here: **JP** canted half-ways on its side. The lazy **JP**. Only there'd been nothing lazy about the people the brand stood for.

It seemed as if hours had passed before he could draw his breath again. He alternated running his fingers through his hair. Slowly, he sank and knelt between the graves, giving in to emotions he had buried—rage, anguish, loneliness, and grief. Then came the hate.

He wanted to cry, but there were no tears to be had. Instead, low moans escaped from his lips, until at last, his awareness of his surroundings became clear once more—the ghosts of its past having receded.

He picked nervously at a few stray weeds that had sprouted in each of the plots. "Mama? Pa? It's me. It's Buster."

As he recited their names, his brow furrowed questioningly. Looking to the left of his father's grave, then to the right of his mother's grave, he did not see what he knew should be near. He stood, then backed away from the graves.

There should have been three graves, not two. Three. His stomach began churning again. Where was Tillie's grave? He prowled for ten feet on either side of the graves, but nothing changed. There were still only two crosses.

Walking around the place that had once been his home and trying to figure out the meaning behind his find, set his head to throbbing. He picked up a large stone from a rock pile that had once been part of a fireplace, and chucked it angrily, as hard and high as he could. As it landed with a thunk, he heard Hank's mocking voice screaming at him: "Ya'll find out. Ya'll see! Ya don't know everthin'. "

"I can't think no more. I need something' to eat." After filling the coffee pot from the stream, he poured the last of the coffee grounds into it and placed it carefully into the fire.

As he waited for the coffee to boil, he tried to sort his rambling, tumbling, twisting thoughts:

First off, I'm in terrible need of new clothes. Winter's comin' on I could use a jacket and breeches. Boots is a must. *Where's Tillie?* Gloves I need gloves. I could do with a real good bath too. Mebbe a haircut.

Is she alive?

I need to stock up on vittles.

How old would she be now?

I'm out of Arbuckle's and hardtack.

Lonely Wind said she saw the bodies of a man an' a woman an' a little girl but they were dead they were dead. I was the only one alive an' she had to get me out of here fast in case whoever done it might come back.

I sure could do with a hot meal sleep in a clean bed with clean sheets I need supplies.

Tillie, where are ya girl? Are ya thirteen? Fourteen? I don' know. I. Don'. Know. I can't remember.

Buster chewed on the last of his jerky as he stared into the ashes of the almost dead fire. He washed the coffee pot, then spread his one-of-a-kind long coat on a grassy spot. Amigo gave a nervous nicker when he heard the sound it made when being unrolled, and moved to the far side of the clearing. Its odor repelled the horse.

Strolling around his creation, Buster studied it thoughtfully. The coat was beginning to show signs of wear and tear from the folding and unfolding. One of the seams was coming apart.

He spoke out loud to Amigo, "Guess I have to get some more sinew an' reinforce that. Mebbe replace the whole panel? Kinda spiff it up before I wear it one more time. For the last time. It don't smell all that good anymore either. Phew. Ya kin smell me comin' a mile away."

That last thought made him giggle, then cackle, then finally, laugh uproariously. He doubled over, clutching at his mid-section, and laughed for a long time because it felt good to laugh. Then, he stopped as suddenly as he had started. His eyes squinted maliciously.

"Let's us go to town, Amigo. We'll make us a new travois for Cranston from some of that corral fence when we get back. It'll be fittin'.

This'll make a right nice base camp. An' when we're done with our task, we can head home to Lonely Wind and Baby Paul from here. That's what we'll do."

He kicked dirt onto his campfire, saddled Amigo, threw two empty saddlebags over the horse's withers, slung an old war bag onto its rump, swung onto the saddle, and headed for Tres Marias.

SEVENTEEN

A SHOCK IN TRES MARIAS

His hair retrimmed to the shoulder length of mourning, his face still stinging from the barber's razor, and the aroma of lye soap emanating, Buster opened the door to the Hughes' Emporium in Tres Marias, New Mexico. The array of items available stunned him—clothes, canned goods, pot and pans, sewing items, lamps and lamp oil—everything he needed, and more. He had plenty in his poke for just about anything he wanted.

The store keep called down from the ladder he was standing on, "Morning, mister. You lookin' for anything special?"

"I need some clothes an' some grub."

"You'll find the ready-to-wear toward the back of the store, and the new shirts and jeans in the next aisle over. If you have a list of the other things you want you can give it to me or speak what you need, and I'll get them for you. Do you know what size clothes you wear?"

Embarrassed at the telling, Buster mumbled, "I shorely do not."

"No matter. Try them on until you find something that comes close to fitting. There's a tailor down the street if you want to have any of your garments tailored."

"Have 'em what?"

"If you want them to fit better."

"Oh. Mebbe. I don' know. I'll go see if I kin find me somethin', if that's all right," Buster answered, wanting to get out of this conversation as fast as possible.

"You go right ahead. If you need any help, my name's Hughes, Elbert Hughes. Pro-pri-et-or, at your service."

"Yessir, Mr. Hughes. Thank you kindly."

Strolling around the aisles, Buster fingered the material on bolts of cloth, shaking his head in wonder at the differently colored candy sticks and jars of brightly colored penny candies, arrayed to tempt the youngsters accompanying their parents. Buster pictured Lonely Wind's and Baby Paul's reactions when he brought them these gifts, then felt foolish at the idea.

Wiping those thoughts from his mind, he strolled over to the tables where men's shirts and jackets were piled. As he picked over an array of pants, the bell over the door jingled and Mr. Hughes greeted his new customer, "Morning, Miss Tillie. How are you today?"

"I'm fine, thank you. And you?" The young girl's voice was light, cheerful with a friendly lilt.

As soon as the name "Tillie" was uttered, Buster's mouth went dry and his heart began to gallop. Peeking around the corner of a stack of men's jeans, he tried to see the girl's reflection in the mirror that hung high on the wall behind the main counter. The poke bonnet she wore hid her face, but from her size he guessed her to be about twelve, or so. Maybe thirteen?

Hughes finished sorting a row of canned peaches and began working his way carefully down the ladder. "I'm mighty fine. What can I do for you?"

"Pa would like you to fill this order for us and have it delivered to the ranch this afternoon, if that's possible?"

"Hmm, this is a large order. I think I have just what you want, but if not, would it be all right if I substituted an item or two, if need be?"

Buster's thoughts careened into one another:

It can't be her. Can it?

Naw, you're only hopin'.

Two graves. Not three.

But she's the right age, mebbe.

It's a coincidence. Too much to hope fer.

Why not?

"Oh, and Ma says to ask when will you be getting some new material. She wants to make curtains for the kitchen."

"You tell your ma that when it comes in, I'll send our boy out to your place to let her know."

"Thank you, Mister Hughes, I will."

As soon as the girl left the store, Buster moved quickly to where Hughes stood behind the counter.

"All right then, young man. Did you find anything to your liking?"

"Uh, yeah, I did. But first, kin ya tell me who that young lady is? Her name?" Buster coughed, and tried to clear his throat. His mouth was still dry.

"That's Tillie Cranston. Pretty young thing. There's a sad story, if I ever heard one. Her parents was killed oh, five, six year back now. A raiding party —young man? Are you all right? Your face is white as chalk!"

Buster's eyes blurred, his body swayed, and he grabbed onto the counter for support.

"Here here now. You sit yourself down. I'll get you some water." Hughes ran to a barrel of water, filled a tin cup, and raced to where Buster sat.

"Drink this, and I'll get you more." Mr. Hughes wiped his hands on his white apron, waiting for Buster to finish, then refilled the cup, and stood ready, just in case.

Buster felt the need to apologize, to say something, anything, to cover his confusion. "I'm sorry, sir. Haven't eaten any breakfast. Guess I'm hungry."

"There's a café two doors down from here, and they'll make anything you want. Good eats."

Buster drank the second cup of water, wiped his mouth on the back of his hand, then dried his hand on his pants. His vision had cleared, but at the mention of food his stomach gurgled, and he realized he was hungrier now than he had been in weeks— maybe months.

"I think I'll take ya up on that an' get me somethin' to eat. I'll come back after I eat, but before I go kin ya tell me the rest of the story 'bout that little girl?"

"Oh, sure. Well, as I was saying, about five, six, year ago now her parents was killed by a raiding party, probably Mescaleros; they come up from Mexico now and again. Anyways when Cranston found her she was hurt real bad—almost dead. She still bears a limp. Her maw and paw were dead, and their cabin was burnt, most of the stock run off. Hear tell that there was a son, 'bout 18 or so, but he was never found. Lots of speculation on his disappearance. Maybe the Indians took him. Who knows? Anyways, Mr. and Mrs. Cranston took Tillie in an' are raisin' her as their daughter, never having' had any children of their own.

"Fine people they are. They have a huge cattle ranch about

twenty miles or so outside of town. I didn't know the other family. Johnson, I think their name was, but I'm not sure 'bout that. I just took over this store a couple of years ago, so I'm just passing on town gossip."

Buster let Mr. Hughes ramble on as he tried to make sense of all he'd just heard. He needed to think about this turn of events, he needed to get some food in his belly, and he needed to plan his next moves.

"Uh excuse me sir. If ya don't mind, I'll just go an' find the café an' I'll come back later an' finish gittin' my supplies. Thanks kindly fer the water."

"Are you sure you're all right? You still look a little funny."

"I'm fine. Jes' need some food. Thanks fer your concern. Be back later."

As Buster was leaving another customer arrived and Hughes greeted the new arrival with friendly familiarity, but not before calling out, "See you later, young man."

EIGHTEEN

THE PLAN CHANGES

Buster chose a seat at an empty table in a corner of the café. The waitress tried to be friendly but he didn't feel much like talking, so she took his order, shrugged at his indifference, and moved to serve another customer.

He stared at the red-and-white checkered tablecloth, his mind whirling with doubt and questions. His lonely existence had made talking to himself a necessity. It had been just him, Amigo, the dying, or those who could not answer, and the voices.

Sometimes those inner voices could be very insistent, and argumentative:

She called them Ma and Pa, but they're not. Ma an' Pa are lying' out there. Cold.

But how do ya really know that's truly Tillie?

What if it's not?

What if it is? What are ya gonna do? One minute ya didn't have a family, and the next, ya do. It's not simple anymore. It's gettin' complicated.

No, it's not.

There's Tillie to consider. Ya go out to Cranston's ranch, tell Tillie the true story, an' take her back with ya to Arizona Territory. Take her back an' introduce her to Lonely Wind and Baby Paul.

But not before you kill Cranston. Remember? Ya have to take him back so he kin spend eternity with Hank an' the others. Ya have to stick to the plan.

Are you stupid enough to think —

The waitress, who was standing at the edge of his table, interrupted his anguished thinking. He looked up at her with a puzzled expression.

"I said, here's your steak and potatoes. You musta been daydreaming. I'll bring your bread in a minute. More coffee?"

"Uh, yeah. Please."

Buster stopped his one-man debate long enough to dig into his food. He ate fast, ravenously, and noisily—table manners forgotten. A man and his wife sitting at the table opposite him raised their eyebrows and shook their heads in disgust, but he paid them no notice. He focused on one thing only—*the plan*—and implementing it as soon as possible.

NINETEEN

THE REUNION

The morning after his trip to Tres Marias, Buster crouched in front of the fire waiting for the coffee to boil. The *plan* and Tillie were the only things he could think about. He'd run the scenario in his mind so many times during the night that he hadn't slept much, but sleep didn't matter now. Only the *plan* mattered:

I'll have breakfast, then I'll go get Tillie, c'mon back here, we'll say goodbye to Ma and Pa an' head fer Arizona Territory.

No, that's not it. I have to find me a snake er two, then I'll go get Tillie, kill Cranston, and his wife too if I have to. No. I'll kill the wife but leave her here. No women in the tomb but Lonely Wind. I'll take Tillie and we'll head for Arizona Territory.

But what about Jupiter?

What about him? He'll come willingly. I won't have no trouble with him.

Yeah, but there'll be you on Amigo with the body on the travois, an' Tillie on her horse, Jupiter an' his young'ns —

He giggled. *That's some wagon train.*

Tillie won't go for it ya know.

She won't have a choice.

But, what if —

His thoughts flew, and his debates continued. With his mind busily engaged, he didn't hear the buckboard, or the jangling of the mules' harness, coming up behind him, nor did he hear the distinct sound of a cartridge being racked into the chamber of a Winchester.

"Stan' up and turn 'round slow like, hands in the air. Yo is trespassin' on Cranston lan'. "

Buster did as he was told, turning toward the voice, saying nothing. He stared at the large black man standing next to the wagon, a rifle aimed at his mid-section. Seated on the buckboard was his sister, Tillie. He was sure now that it was her. She looked too much like Ma not to be. Her eyes were Johansson blue.

"Tillie. It's me! It's Buster! Don't you remember me? I'm yer brother," he shouted, running toward the wagon.

"Stay where you are," the man holding the weapon ordered, aiming the rifle at Buster's mid-section to prove his intent.

Buster stopped running, standing stock-still, anxiety contorting his face, his hands clenching and unclenching nervously. Then, softly, he began singing Tillie's favorite song. *"Put yer little foot, put yer little foot, put yer little foot right—"*

"Buster? No, it can't be! Is it you? Really you?" She jumped from the wagon and ran toward him.

"No, Miss Tillie. Don' you go near him! Don' you move young fella. I kin shoot fast and straight. I was in the Union army. Miss Tillie, you come back here now."

"It's okay, Jerusalem. He *is* my brother. It's really him."

But as Jerusalem watched his young mistress clutching the scrawny trespasser, while both cried tears of joy and sorrow, an uneasy feeling crept through him, and he kept his Winchester at the ready.

TWENTY

JERUSALEM

During the next few hours, as the two sat at the edges of their parents' graves, Buster rambled and stuttered his way through the past the past five years: Lonely Wind and Baby Paul, snakes, cattle drives, murders, catacombs and, *the plan.*

Tillie had held her brother's hands tightly through the first part of his story but when he described how he stalked, then found, then wiped out any trace of four human beings, she'd let go of them, burying hers in the folds of her apron. She twined and untwined her unseen fingers nervously. Almost imperceptibly she moved away from that which had now become repugnant to her.

If Buster noticed his sister's withdrawal he did not react, continuing to recite his gruesome tale. Apparently he also had not noticed the look of horror that crawled quietly across her face.

As his story unfolded, the last of Buster's presence in reality skittered away and his immersion into his dark, lonely world was almost complete. It was familiar and comfortable. The thought never crossed his mind that others would construe the world he'd been consumed by as bizarre. He could not comprehend that a listener would know that the man telling this tale was almost totally insane.

There was pride in his voice when he spoke about how he had first captured the animal from whose hide the duster was created and how, with Lonely Wind's help, he had sewn it together with the precision of a tailor. Suddenly, he leapt up, ran over to his bedroll and gently, lovingly, removed the duster and the hatband.

"Wait 'til I show ya this, Tillie. I reckon ya'll be amazed at what ya see." Buster took his prized possessions and ran into the shadows of a copse of trees standing near the graves.

Neither Tillie, nor Jerusalem was able to see him clearly until he emerged from the shadows into the sunlight, undulating and swiveling his hips. He had adopted this attempt at a writhing style of walking—almost gliding—during his third murder, so that he would be more like *El Cascabel*. As he snapped his head from side to side the rattles on the hatband sounded. Amigo and the mules reacted by nervously pawing the ground.

Tillie rose from her kneeling position, standing rigid with fear. As Buster slithered toward his sister, he described the glee he felt at finding, then watching his enemies die. He laughed loudly, as if he were telling a funny joke, describing the horrible manner and suffering involved in their dying.

That his sister did not join in his laughter did not bother him. The joy at finding her was overshadowed by his desire to impress her with how he had taken revenge on their enemies. He would have been heartbroken at her reaction. After all, he had done it all for them. For Ma. For Pa. For her.

And finally, after *the plan* was fully revealed, and his intentions to kill Pa Cranston fully discussed, Tillie realized that the brother she had once known, the brother whom she had missed and for whom she had grieved was no more. He had sunk into a world into which she could not, would not, follow. Buster Johansson was as dead to her as if he had died five years ago.

The abomination that stood in front of her, dressed in an ungodly fashion that reeked with death's smell, looked a lot like the pa she had known as a little girl. It was certainly not the brother who had carried her on his shoulders, who had made cornhusk dolls for her, who played silly childhood games with her. Even at this tender age, she recognized pure evil. She saw him as the monster he had become.

The young girl, who had just briefly found her lost brother at the graves of her parents—the graves she had lovingly tended over the years, at first with the help of the Cranstons and now with the help of her friend and companion, Jerusalem—wished the man who called himself her brother had died with her parents.

She wanted him to stop telling his dreadful tales of murder and death. She wanted to tell him that he was wrong about what had happened to her and their parents.

She wanted to tell him what Pa Cranston had told her and anyone else who'd asked: that Mescaleros had raided her ma and pa's ranch, but had been run off by Hank and some of Pa Cranston's ranch hands who'd just happened to be in the area, and who had found her badly injured, her leg broken, so they'd taken her and the big bull Jupiter back to the Cranstons so they could bring her back to good health and raise her as their very own, and the big bull would be safe and live out the rest of his years as he was meant to;

That he'd tried to find her brother, but had never discovered what had happened to him, and that she couldn't remember very much about that day at all.

But Buster had gone on and on without stopping, his eyes glistening, his laughter becoming more raucous.

As she slowly backed away from this madman, she looked to her friend for help; to the friend who had not taken his eyes off of her from the minute they'd arrived. She knew she was as dear to Jerusalem as if she were his own daughter.

When the Civil War ended, he had traveled west, finding employment with the Cranstons as a ranch hand. That changed on the day he had rescued her from an angry and charging seed bull known as Jupiter. Flowers in hand, she had wandered into the field where the prized animal was grazing, wanting to feed him as she had many times before. But on that day, Jupiter didn't recognize the little girl he had known for so long. On that day, his mind was on breeding. He wanted no attention from humans.

Snorting with rage, he thundered toward Tillie. When Jupiter saw the other human racing toward the girl he stopped, pawed the ground and threw his head back, bellowing in anger at the intrusion. Jerusalem picked up the tiny girl, moving quietly and deliberately away from the huge beast, who lost interest in the two humans as a cow wandered into his view.

From that day forward, Jerusalem was given the job of her bodyguard and companion. He never left her side and would gladly, as had been shown, have given his life for hers.

Now standing at the head of the team hitched to the buckboard, his eyes shifted from Miss Tillie to her brother. He'd heard the words pouring from Buster's mouth, and was as filled with shock and revulsion at his performance as Tillie. *I knows what crazy is, and that un's crazy-loco.*

As the afternoon shadows grew longer and Buster's reality grew shorter, Jerusalem knew he didn't have much time. When he saw his young mistress look pleadingly to him for help, he knew he needed to act immediately.

"Miss Tillie, we needs to go home now. I knows your parents will be worryin' 'bout you. We been here long enough and if we don' leave soon, your pa is goin' to be lookin' for us with some of the boys."

At the sound of Jerusalem's voice, Buster, who had become oblivious to his audience, hissed in a snake-like warning. He turned toward the man whose words told him he was going to be robbed of the sister he just found. His mind flashed with caution: *That man's goin' to interfere with the plan. Ya cain't let that happen.*

Buster was wearing the coat, but did not have the assistant he had used four times before. *El Cascabel*, and the fangs that had delivered death for him, was nowhere around. He'd have to use the next best thing: the sharp knife he'd used to cut off the reptile's head and rattles and skin its carcass would serve well. In his mind, the sharpness of the knife blade equated to the sharpness of the snake's bite.

Reaching inside the duster, he unsheathed the knife from its place on his belt and in his mind's eye, saw the snake's mouth opening wide, fangs extended, ready to strike. The knife in his hand had become his fangs. He had at last become *El Cascabel*.

With serpent-like awareness, his reality shifted quickly from the past to the present. He frowned, realizing that Tillie was no longer standing as near to him as she had been—she had almost reached the buckboard. His sister's pretty young face, once filled with love for him, was now filled with loathing and disgust and one other emotion. Fear. His beloved Tillie was afraid of him. *How kin that be?*

"Tillie? Girl? What's the matter? Why're you afraid of me. C'mon back here, next to me." His voice was whiny and pleading, but his eyes had narrowed in anger.

"I did this all for you…for us… and Ma… and Pa. Nobody else coulda done it. Nobody else *woulda* done it. It had to be done. They needed to be taught a lesson. All of them needed learnin'.

"I want you to go with me so's you kin meet Lonely Wind and Baby Paul. They're waitin' for us. They'll be so surprised. They thought ya was dead. Like I did. But ya ain't."

Tillie's backward retreat had placed her between her brother and her protector. She was unaware that she was blocking the clear shot that Jerusalem had counted on.

"Miss Tillie, why don' you git up in the wagon *now,* so's we can gets home for supper. Your ma's got sumpin' good planned." Jerusalem's low voice had remained steady, calm, and even, but his emphasis on the word *now* caught the girl's attention and she responded immediately.

It also caught Buster's attention. When he saw the last member of his family stepping into the wagon, preparing to leave him—again—he ran in leaping bounds toward the buckboard, knife raised high.

His crazy leaps had brought him almost directly in front of the mules. They shook their heads, as if responding to the threat. Their harness jingled, the wagon stopped. Buster's eyes flitted wildly between his sister and the stranger holding a gun.

Brushing his chin and right ear against his right shoulder, he frowned with indecision; his face contorted with rage. The stranger was interfering with the plan, but so was his sister.

"She's not your ma. Our ma's a-lyin' over there with Pa. An' if you say that she is, then maybe you should be a-lyin' with them like you was supposed to be in the first place."

Tillie pleaded, "Buster! No! Stop, please. I love you."

"If you loved me, you'd go with me. You'd help me kill Cranston. You're like everyone else. Everyone else has left me. Not this time. You're comin' with me, one way or another!"

A shaft of sunlight glinted off the knife blade as the madman made his choice. He sprang to his left, circled around the mules and headed toward the sister he had once treasured, who now sat shrieking in terror; her screams sending panicked birds into swift flight, squawking and cawing. Amigo bolted from the clearing into the woods.

The Winchester blasted, catching Buster in mid-leap, bullets finding the places in his back that bore the scars of old gunshot wounds. As Buster crumpled to the ground, Jerusalem grabbed the mules' harness to steady the nervous animals. The clearing had become still, almost peaceful.

Jerusalem swung onto the seat and began apologizing. "Miss Tillie, I'm sorry. He was gonna kill you. I hadda do it. Please, Miss Tillie, don' you be mad at Jerusalem."

Sobbing into her apron, she answered in a muffled voice, "Oh, Jerusalem, how can I be mad at you?" Raising her tear-stained face, she looked gratefully at her dearest friend, "You saved my life. Again. Thank you, thank you."

She had not left the wagon, and could not bring herself to look down at her brother's body, lying in a twisted heap near the buckboard's step. It was just as well. During his death throes, the duster had totally wrapped around his body, his hat had jammed onto his head, his body had curved end to end. In repose, he now resembled the animal he had strived to become.

The little girl's tears flowed again. "What are we going to do with him?"

"I'll come back tomorrow and bury him next to your ma and pa, if that's okay wid you. It's gettin' too dark to see now."

"Do you think he'll be all right here? I mean —"

"I'll put some stones on him, so it'll keep the . . . you know, away . . . so's he won' be bothered."

Tillie spoke softly, "And I'll paint some rocks to put around his grave and, in spring, I'll plant some of those yellow flowers so his grave can look like Ma's and Pa's." Through fresh tears she added, "I'll make another cross."

TWENTY ONE

THREE GRAVES

Jerusalem used soot-blackened fireplace stones to temporarily cover the body, then turned the buckboard around and headed for home. Amigo, who had wandered back into the clearing, was tethered to the wagon's rear.

"Jerusalem?"

"Yes'm."

"I wanted to tell Buster that he was wrong, but he didn't give me a chance. I wanted to tell him what Pa Cranston told me, that it was Mescaleros who killed our ma and pa, and not Hank and the other men like Buster thought.

"Pa and Ma Cranston have been so good to me. Raising me as their own. Pa looked for Buster and even put out a reward for finding him, but no one ever saw him again. The Cranstons wouldn't lie to me, would they."

The little girl was so sure of the answer that her remark was not made in the form of a question, but as a statement of fact.

Tillie reached into the back of the wagon, found her shawl and wrapped it around her, warding off the October evening's chill. Before turning to face forward, she looked back toward the mound of stones, and murmured, "You're home now, brother. I love you."

"Miss Tillie, yo needs to forgit what happened this afternoon an' jus' 'member yo brother as he used to be."

"I'll try, Jerusalem. I'll try." She moved closer to her friend, lacing her small arm through his, and resting her head on his shoulder. "It's getting colder, isn't it? Pa said winter's going to come early this year."

She paused, before saying in a small voice, "Maybe it'll snow for Christmas."

* * *

GLOSSARY OF SORTS

A bit of an explanation for those unfamiliar with some of the words used:

Burden basket: As is implied, it was a basket used for carrying and storage

Parfleche (pronounced per-flesh): a rawhide bag originally used by Canadian-French fur trappers for storing dried meat and pemmican and eventually adopted by Native Americans

Travois (pronounced trav-wah): another Canadian-French term, a frame used to drag loads

Wickiup (pronounced wicki-up): shelter/housing made from trees and branches

More information on Apache Women Warriors can be found at:
Arizona Historical Society
949 E. 2nd Street
Tucson, AZ 85719

ABOUT THE AUTHOR

Hailing from the Midwest, Mary Ann Hutchison is a transplanted Wisconsinite who spent over 40 years in the legal field as: a legal secretary, Administrative Assistant for the Pima County Sheriff's Department, Courtroom Clerk and Judicial Administrative Assistant for the Pima County Superior Court.

After retiring she began to seriously put words on paper and writes short stories, memoirs, middle-grade, and suspense stories.

One husband, two spoiled felines, a blended family of six children, 19 grandchildren, and eight great-grandchildren constitute her immediate family.

Her writing family derives from her affiliation with Gecko Gals Ink LLC (five "Tucson authors who are Differently Expertised"), Arizona Mystery Writers (past-Presiding Chair), former member of the Society of Southwestern Authors (former member of its Board of Directors, Coordinator of the Society's media promotion and writing contest), and former member of the Society of Children's Book Writers and Illustrators.

"Rain, Rain, Go Away…" her newest adult suspense novel is available from your local bookstore, Anaphora Literary Press, Amazon.com and Barnes and Noble.com. "Justice is often delayed, but WILL NOT be denied. To those who labor in the judiciary and law enforcement, two things are well known: Time is always of the essence and knowing is one thing, proving it another. It's implicit that no matter their vocation, what they do after hours must shatter the images of what they consistently see and hear.

"*Moochi's Mariachis,* her YA novel, is available from Open Books Press, Amazon.com, Barnes & Noble.com, and as an e-book. With great pride, "Moochi" is now a part of the Tucson Unified School District's Title I ESL Program. A portion of the proceeds of the book is donated to the Arizona Kidney Foundation.

The novella, "Cascabel," an e-book, can be found on Amazon.com and BarnesandNoble.com. The-wide open western frontier in 1865 is the backdrop for chilling revenge and murder.

Her short stories and memoirs are included in "Good Old Days" magazines, "Thanksgiving to Christmas: A Patchwork of Stories," (AWOC.COM Publishing) and Arizona Mystery Writers anthology, "A Way With Murder" (XLibris), and "Gecko Tales" — an e-book available on Amazon.com or from the author.

Her website is: www.bloomincane.com.